SURF VS. TURF

"Dance with me a while, honey!" Dunn yelled.

The barkeep might have managed to get Dunn away from Antonia and off the dance floor without a fight breaking out if he had gotten there first. But Cooley, the burly sailor, reached the scene ahead of him.

"Get your cow-stinkin' paws off of her!" Cooley shouted as he jerked Dunn back. But Dunn's fist was already streaking toward the sailor's jaw. The blow caught the sailor off-balance, but Cooley caught himself and snapped a punch to Dunn's face. Outraged yells went up from the other cowboys in the cantina as they saw one of their own being struck. Curses came from the sailors as they prepared to defend their friend.

"Oh, Lordy," Cappy said to Longarm. "All hell's gonna bust loose now."

Longarm figured the old-timer was right. He didn't want to get involved in it, but as the two opposing groups moved toward each other and fists began to fly, one of the sailors glanced in Longarm's direction and saw the Stetson on the big lawman's head. He bellowed, "Damned cow nurse" and then snatched up a chair and threw it as hard as he could. It went over Longarm's head and smashed into the wall. The shattered pieces fell around him. But the sailor wasn't going to let it go at that. With his hands balled into fists, he charged across the cantina, straight at the man he had picked for his opponent.

Longarm scrambled to his feet and muttered, "Cappy, get out of here!"

"Hell, no!" the old-timer replied. "I ain't never run away from a good scrap!"

TABOR EVANS

LONGARM

AND THE PIRATE'S GOLD

JOVE BOOKS, NEW YORK

This is a work of fiction. Names, characters, places, and incidents either are the product of the author's imagination or are used fictitiously, and any resemblance to actual persons, living or dead, business establishments, events, or locales is entirely coincidental.

LONGARM AND THE PIRATE'S GOLD

A Jove Book / published by arrangement with
the author

PRINTING HISTORY
Jove edition / May 2004

Copyright © 2004 by Penguin Group (USA) Inc.

ISBN: 0-515-13734-0

A JOVE BOOK®
Jove Books are published by The Berkley Publishing Group,
a division of Penguin Group (USA) Inc.,
375 Hudson Street, New York, New York 10014.
JOVE and the "J" design
are trademarks belonging to Penguin Group (USA) Inc.

PRINTED IN THE UNITED STATES OF AMERICA

10 9 8 7 6 5 4 3 2 1

Chapter 1

Longarm had heard the old saying about how when someone was drowning, their entire life passed before their
eyes.

He knew now that wasn't true. He had already swallowed a gutful of water and was going down for the third
time, and he hadn't seen a blamed thing except the blue-
green waves of the Gulf of Mexico as they slapped him
in the face.

Struggling mightily, he managed to get his head above
the surface and gulp down some air. The third time under
hadn't killed him after all. He felt a faint flicker of hope
deep inside him. He wasn't the sort to give up on life.
Not after all the dangers he had gone through over the
years.

Normally he was a good swimmer. But the water was
choppy on the Gulf today. Gray clouds scudded through
the sky, and a strong wind kicked up the waves. The bullet
crease on his shoulder didn't help matters any, either. The
painful wound made it more difficult for him to tread
water.

Longarm shook the wet hair out of his eyes and looked
around. There had to be a boat somewhere close by. He
didn't see any vessels, though. Which way was land? He

turned all the way around in the water, searching for any sign of the Texas coastline.

Nothing. Nothing but angry water and angry skies. He knew he had to do something, had to start swimming before he was completely exhausted, but if he took off in the wrong direction and swam away from the shore, he would seal his doom.

He had known all along there was a good reason why he didn't like ships. When they sank, they left you stranded in the water. That didn't happen on land, with a good horse under a fella. Longarm liked horses, though they could be stubborn brutes sometimes. He wished he had one to ride right now.

You're starting to think crazy, old son, he told himself. A horse wouldn't do him a damned bit of good. He forced himself to concentrate. A seagull's cry made him look up. He saw the bird winging overhead and decided that it was headed for shore. Even a seagull had to come down and land sometime, didn't it?

Longarm began to swim, following the seagull.

Some instinct made him look back. He saw a gray fin cutting sleekly through the water. His jaw tightened in fear and anger.

One old saying *was* true, he thought: Things were never so bad that they couldn't get worse.

"Aw, Billy, you know I don't much like the ocean," Longarm had said a week or so earlier as he frowned at the report Chief Marshal Billy Vail had just passed across the desk in Vail's Denver office.

"I don't care," Vail said. With his balding head and pink cheeks, the chief marshal looked almost cherubic. Most folks wouldn't take him for the veteran star packer he really was. Back in his Texas Ranger days, though, Vail had been a real hell-roarer. He continued, "The Department of the Treasury has asked us for a hand, and we're going to give them one."

Longarm sat back in the red leather chair and cocked

a booted foot on the other knee. He had come into the Federal Building this morning in a pretty good mood after spending the night with a plump, bosomy widow woman of his acquaintance, but Vail had spoiled that in a hurry with this new job.

Taking a cheroot from his vest pocket, Longarm put it in his mouth and chewed on it as he read the report. It came from the Revenue Cutter Service, part of the Department of the Treasury, and concerned the sinking of the vessel *Russell Andrew* in the Gulf of Mexico, off the coast of southern Texas. The main job of revenue cutters was to stop smuggling. The boat had gone down with all hands. Some floating wreckage had been found, but that was all.

"Seems like Treasury would want to investigate this their ownselves," Longarm said as he looked up from the document.

"They want somebody with experience at getting to the bottom of tricky cases. That would be you, Custis."

Longarm grunted. "I don't reckon 'getting to the bottom of' is a very good choice of words when you're talking about the ocean, Billy. That's just what I'm worried about."

Vail ignored the comment. "You'll start for Corpus Christi right away. That's the closest port to the spot where that cutter went down."

"How do we know the blamed boat didn't just spring a leak? Or go down in a squall?"

"You didn't read the report close enough," Vail said, pointing a pudgy finger. "Check the condition of the debris that was found."

Longarm frowned as he scanned the words, looking for the information Vail indicated. The frown deepened as he saw what the chief marshal was talking about.

"Some of the planks were charred, like they'd been burned before the ship sank." Longarm's teeth tightened on the cheroot. "You're right, Billy. That ain't natural. Somebody set that cutter on fire."

3

Vail nodded. "It's your job to find out who and why and see that they answer for it."

"How many men were on the boat?" Longarm asked quietly.

"It carried a crew of eighteen."

"And there were no survivors?"

Vail shook his head. "None."

Longarm sighed and then tossed the report back onto Vail's desk. "You want me to leave right away, you said?"

"That's right."

Longarm stood up. He was a tall, rangy, muscular man with dark brown hair, sweeping longhorn mustache, and a sharply planed face cured by the sun to the color of old saddle leather. He wore a brown tweed suit with a vest and carried a Colt .45 in a crossdraw rig on his left hip. He had been a deputy United States marshal for a long time and was good at his job.

"I'll be going, then," he said as he picked up his flat-crowned, snuff-brown Stetson and settled it on his head.

"Henry has your travel vouchers," Vail told him.

Longarm nodded curtly and left the chief marshal's private office. Nothing more needed to be said. Vail knew he would do the job—or die trying.

Vail's secretary was a pale, spectacle-wearing young man who had a running feud with Longarm. Longarm had never been able to decide if Henry liked him and was just covering it up, or if the fella really couldn't stand him. As Longarm came out of Vail's office, Henry turned from his typewriter and gave Longarm a stack of travel vouchers to be filled out.

"Off to sea, are we?" he asked with a smile.

"Go back to playing your typewriter," Longarm grumbled as he tucked the vouchers away inside his coat. "Billy ought to send you on this job, old son. Reckon you'd be right at home on the ocean, seeing as how you're so wet behind the ears."

Henry just shook his head and chuckled. "Is that the best you can do? You're slipping, Marshal."

4

Longarm clamped his teeth on the cheroot and stalked out of the office. The four-eyed little son of a buck was right, he thought. He'd have to work on that.

A combination of railroad and stagecoach lines carried Longarm to the Gulf Coast of Texas. His job had brought him to the area several times before, including one case where he had run into a bunch of cannibalistic Indians. He still shivered when he thought about what those Karankawas had done to one fella. Of course, the hombre had deserved it, but still . . .

The humidity down here was always oppressive, he thought as he climbed out of a stagecoach in downtown Corpus Christi, especially to someone who was accustomed to the drier air of the mountain and desert climes where he spent most of his time. He took off his hat and sleeved sweat from his forehead.

Corpus Christi was laid out on the south side of Nueces Bay, with some of the town on a little bluff that overlooked the bay and the docks, and the rest of the settlement curving around on the waterfront itself. As in all towns this far south in Texas, a lot of the population was of Mexican descent, and that influence showed in the architecture. Longarm saw a lot of adobe buildings with red tile roofs.

The city was a seaport, though, with the Gulf of Mexico opening out wide to the east and leading to the Atlantic Ocean. That meant there were people of all nationalities passing through Corpus Christi all the time. When a fella walked down the street he might hear a British accent or somebody jabbering in Turkish or cussing in Russian or German.

The stage station wasn't far from the docks. As a breeze blew in his face, Longarm tasted the salt on his lips from the ocean. It was hot and humid here, sure enough, but one thing you could say for the place was that there was always some wind to keep the air stirred up.

5

As he took his warbag, saddle, and Winchester from the boot, he asked the station manager where he could find a decent hotel and a good place to get a drink. The manager had come out to supervise the hostlers as they changed teams. He didn't hesitate in answering Longarm's question. He had probably been asked similar queries countless times.

"Same place will do you for both, mister. The Nueces Hotel is right up the street, and it has a good barroom attached to it."

Longarm nodded. "Much obliged."

"Of course, if you're looking for a place a little more colorful," the man added, "you can always try Miguel's. It's a cantina a few blocks down Water Street. I don't know that I'd advise it, though. It can be a rough place."

"Thanks for the advice. I'll probably stick with the Nueces, though. I'm a peaceable man, never look for trouble."

"That's a good way to be, friend."

Longarm grinned to himself as he turned away. With his saddle balanced on his left shoulder and his warbag and rifle in his right hand, he walked up Water Street to the Nueces Hotel.

The hotel was a large, two-story frame building made of heavy, whitewashed planks. It had a deep verandah along the front that faced the ocean. Longarm imagined the verandah would be a pleasant place of an evening, when the Gulf breeze cooled off some.

He went inside and registered for a room, was given one on the second floor. He went up and dropped his gear on the bed, washed off the dust of the stagecoach ride, and put on a clean shirt. Then he went back downstairs and ambled through the lobby. An arched doorway led into a dim barroom. Curtains were pulled over all the windows. Fans hung down from the ceiling and turned lazily.

Longarm went to the mahogany bar and said to the

man behind it, "You wouldn't happen to have any Maryland rye, would you?"

The man grinned, and even in the faint light, a gold tooth gleamed. "This is a seaport bar, my friend. If anybody in the world drinks it, we have it. Tom Moore be all right with you?"

Longarm grinned back at the bartender. "That's more than all right."

The bartender took two glasses from under the bar and splashed amber liquid in both of them. He left the bottle on the bar. "First one's on the house, and I'll have one with you, if you don't mind."

"Be my pleasure," Longarm assured the man. A friendly, talkative bartender often was one of the best sources of information for a gent in his line of work. He picked up one of the glasses and said, "To your health."

"And yours."

They tossed back the drinks, and Longarm licked his lips in appreciation. "That's the real stuff," he said.

"Wouldn't try to fool you . . . especially since I took a drink of it myself."

Longarm chuckled and felt an instinctive liking for the bartender. He was about to try to steer the conversation toward the sunken revenue cutter when the bartender looked past him and frowned.

"Oh, Lord, here comes trouble," the man said in a low voice.

Longarm heard a heavy step and turned to look at the entryway between the hotel lobby and the barroom. It was filled at the moment by a huge man with massive shoulders and hamlike hands that hung low at his sides. With the light at the man's back, Longarm couldn't tell much about his features. He could see the long black beard, though.

The bartender reached under the bar and brought out a bung starter. He laid it on the bar and said, "I don't want any trouble in here, Larribee."

"Won't be any trouble, mate," the newcomer rumbled

in a British accent. He shuffled farther into the bar and looked around. "Got any o' my crew in here?"

"Haven't seen any of them all day," the bartender said. "Why don't you try down at Miguel's?"

"Just come from there. Rounded up some o' the laya-bouts, but there's still several of 'em missin'."

"Well, they're not here."

The bushy head nodded. The cap jammed down on the rumpled thatch of black hair looked ridiculously small, but that was only because Larribee's head was so big.

"I can see that." Larribee squinted at Longarm and studied him from boots to Stetson. "You're a likely lookin' specimen. Ever think about goin' to sea?"

Longarm had been on several seagoing vessels and had nearly lost his life every time. He had even been shang-haied into a ship's crew. He didn't explain all that, how-ever. Instead, as he picked up the bottle of Maryland rye and poured himself another drink, he just shook his head and said, "Not interested, Cap'n."

Larribee grunted. "You damned cowboys are all alike. If there ain't a horse involved, it ain't worth doin'." He turned back toward the entrance to the hotel lobby.

At that moment, a man started into the barroom. He stopped short at the sight of Larribee. If he had been quicker, he would have scuttled back out of sight. But before he could move, Larribee thundered, "Fitzgerald! There ye be! Stand fast, damn you!"

Larribee moved quicker than seemed possible for a man of his bulk. He lunged forward, grabbed the collar of the luckless Fitzgerald, and jerked the man toward him. Larribee pivoted, and in his anger, he flung Fitzgerald away from him.

That sent Fitzgerald flying straight at a startled Long-arm.

Chapter 2

Longarm had no chance to get out of the way. Fitzgerald crashed into him and knocked him back against the bar. The liquor in the glass spilled all over the front of Longarm's shirt and the edge of the hardwood dug painfully into his back. He caught hold of Fitzgerald with his free hand to keep the man from bouncing off and falling to the floor.

A frightened, weathered face peered up at him. Fitzgerald was a head shorter than Longarm and considerably older. White hair fell to his shoulders, and he had a beard of the same shade, except for yellow tobacco stains around the mouth.

Longarm put the now empty glass on the bar and kept his other hand on Fitzgerald's arm until he was sure the old-timer was steady enough to stand up on his own. Behind the bar, the bartender brandished the bung starter and said, "I told you I didn't want trouble, Larribee."

"My apologies," Larribee said, but he didn't sound much like he meant it. "I lost my temper for a minute when I saw this old scut. He's been duckin' me all day."

"That ain't true!" Fitzgerald protested. "I got no reason to hide from you, Larribee."

In the tangle of black beard, Larribee's teeth gleamed in a fierce grin. "No? What about that voyage you signed on for, and now you're tryin' to get out of it?"

"I never signed on for no voyage! I paid Mr. Thorpe all the money I owe him. You got no call to shanghai me, Larribee."

Larribee's big hands clenched into fists. "I don't like bein' accused o' such things. I never shanghaied a man yet. Not one!" He took a step toward Fitzgerald.

Longarm moved forward and put out his left hand, blocking Larribee's path. "Hold on there, old son," he said. "This fella's too old for you to go swinging those fists at him. You're liable to bust him up mighty bad."

"Takin' his part, are you?" Larribee asked with a sneer.

Longarm's voice was deceptively mild as he replied, "Well, I did spill a drink of perfectly good Maryland rye because of you."

Larribee didn't wait to be challenged any more. He growled a curse and launched a huge fist at Longarm's head.

Longarm ducked the punch and shoved Fitzgerald to the side, out of harm's way. He stepped forward and hooked a blow into Larribee's belly.

"Damn it, no fighting!" the bartender yelled.

It was too late for that warning. Longarm's fist landed solidly in Larribee's midsection.

It was like punching an oak plank.

Longarm grimaced and aimed a blow at Larribee's chin instead, hoping it would be more vulnerable, but the man blocked it with a left and jabbed a right at Longarm's head. Longarm leaned to the side, but he couldn't get completely out of the way of the punch. Larribee's fist grazed the side of his head and staggered him.

"I'll help you, mister!" Fitzgerald yelled. He snatched up a chair at a nearby table and swung it at Larribee's head, ignoring the bartender's howl of protest. The chair crashed over Larribee's skull and knocked his cap off.

Larribee gave a little shake of his head in response to the blow, as if a gnat were bothering him. He swung a backhand at Fitzgerald and clipped the old man. Fitzgerald sailed backward and crashed down on a table, snapping its legs.

The distraction provided by the old-timer had given Longarm a chance to set himself. As Larribee turned back toward him, Longarm crashed a fist into the bearded jaw. The punch had more effect than the last one. Larribee staggered back a step.

Longarm tried to follow up on his momentary advantage. He bored in, ignoring Larribee's body as a lost cause. He knew he couldn't inflict any damage there. Instead he peppered a quick combination to Larribee's face. The punches hurt enough to draw a roar of rage from the huge man. He lunged toward Longarm.

As Larribee's ape-like arms went around him, Longarm knew he had made a mistake by getting too close to the man. He tried to grab a breath before the arms closed on him like a vise, but he was only half-successful. The air in his lungs wouldn't last long.

The bear hug crushed Longarm until he felt like his ribs were about to collapse. His arms were pinned to his sides. He felt his feet come off the floor as Larribee leaned back. Longarm was no lightweight. It took a lot of strength to lift him like that.

His face was only inches from Larribee's. The man's breath was sour with fish and beer. Longarm gritted his teeth, ducked his head down between his shoulders as much as he could, and butted Larribee in the face. The top of Longarm's head impacted Larribee's prominent nose.

Larribee screeched in pain as blood spurted. Longarm had found his weak spot. He butted Larribee again and felt the bear hug loosen. Longarm was able to tear his arms free. He brought up both fists, slamming them like sledgehammers into Larribee's ears.

Larribee stumbled back a step as he let go of Longarm. The big lawman was off-balance, too, but he caught himself and drove forward, lowering his shoulder. The collision sent Larribee reeling backward toward the bar.

11

Longarm kept up the pressure, pushing hard with his feet against the sawdust-sprinkled floor.

Larribee hit the bar and cried out in pain as his momentum bent him backward over it. Longarm spread a hand over his face and shoved it down. The back of Larribee's head cracked against the bar.

Longarm moved back a couple of steps, fists clenched and ready. All the fight had gone out of Larribee, though. He managed to straighten, and he shook his head groggily as he stood there for a moment, swaying. Then, with a sigh, he pitched forward and landed on his face with a mighty crash.

"By the great horn spoon!" the old-timer called Fitzgerald cried out. "I never seen anybody knock out Mauler Larribee before!"

Longarm was breathing hard. His pulse hammered wildly in his head. Caught up in battle frenzy, he wanted to punch somebody else. That was why, when he heard a footstep behind him, he whirled around and whipped up a fist, ready to strike.

He stopped short when he found himself looking at a woman.

She never flinched, and he liked that immediately about her. She just stared back at him with shocking green eyes. Thick masses of dark brown hair tumbled around her head. Her features were a bit too strong for classic beauty, and she had a small cleft in her chin, something that Longarm normally didn't find all that attractive on a woman. On her it looked just fine, though.

She wore canvas trousers that hugged curving hips and legs, and a gray woolen shirt. It wasn't typical female garb, but Longarm could tell by looking at her that she wasn't a typical female.

After a few seconds of strained silence, the woman said, "If you want to punch me, go ahead and try it, mister." The challenge in her voice said that she would do her best to stop him.

Longarm lowered his arm and unclenched his fists.

"Sorry, ma'am," he said tightly. "You sort of snuck up on me."

"I didn't mean to. I just wanted to check on Cappy."

"That's me," Fitzgerald offered as he came forward. "I'm fine, Sandy. Got bounced around a mite, but no harm done."

She gave the old man a fleeting smile. "That's good. Don't call me Sandy." She gestured at the unconscious hulk on the barroom floor and said to Longarm, "You knocked out Larribee?"

"Seemed like the thing to do at the time. It was either that or let him squeeze me to death."

"Yes, Larribee's done things like that before," she said with a nod. "He's a monster, but every time he's killed a man in some drunken brawl, the law has said it was self-defense. I suppose it was. The other men were trying to kill him."

The bartender said, "That didn't happen here. Larribee attacked this fella and started the fight. I'm going to have him locked up." He looked at the handful of bystanders, men who had been drinking in the bar when the trouble started. "Somebody fetch the marshal."

"He should be on his way already," the young woman called Sandy said. "The word went up and down Water Street in a hurry that Larribee was at it again. I heard Cappy was mixed up in it somehow and came to see about him." She looked at Longarm and went on, "I never knew anyone to knock out Larribee before."

Cappy Fitzgerald laughed and said, "That's just what I was sayin', Sandy!"

This time she didn't correct him. Instead she said to Longarm, "Are you a sailor?"

"No, ma'am." He bent to pick up his Stetson from the floor before anybody could step on it.

"I didn't think so." She sounded slightly disappointed. "I take it you're a cowboy?"

"Something like that," he said vaguely. He didn't plan on revealing his identity as a federal lawman unless and

13

until it became necessary. "Before the fight started, Larribee there acted sort of like he might want to hire me for a ship's crew. Did you have the same thing in mind?"

"I can always use good sailors. My name is Sandra Nolan. I own a ship."

"You're the captain?" Longarm asked in surprise.

"No, I just own it. I have a captain who works for me."

It was unusual enough for a woman to own a sailing vessel, he thought. It would have been almost unheard of for a female to be a ship's captain. A lot of sailors wouldn't even set foot on a ship with a woman on board. They regarded it as bad luck.

"Not Larribee, I hope," Longarm said with a smile.

"Not anymore," Sandra Nolan said, again taking him by surprise. "I discharged him six months ago. Since then he's gone to work for Harrison Thorpe."

Longarm recalled Cappy Fitzgerald mentioning someone named Thorpe. He said, "I reckon this fella Thorpe owns a boat, too?"

"A ship," Sandra said. "Several of them, actually. He's what they call a shipping magnate."

A new voice said from the doorway, "Hardly that. I just have a small company with a few vessels. But we're growing."

The man who had spoken strode into the barroom. He was as tall as Longarm, well built but not quite as muscular. He wore a town suit, but his face was tanned and his grip was strong as he thrust out a hand and shook with Longarm. "Harrison Thorpe," he said to introduce himself.

Longarm nodded toward Larribee, who was beginning to stir slightly as consciousness returned to him. "Then this hombre works for you."

"Sad to say that's true," Thorpe agreed with a sigh. He looked at the bartender and went on, "I'll pay for any damages, Ernie."

"Damn right you will," the bartender said. "A chair and a table got busted up."

14

"Send the bill over to my office. I'll take care of it right away."

The bartender nodded, slightly mollified. He was still upset about the fight, though. Longarm doubted if he owned the place, since it was part of the Nueces Hotel, but obviously he was as protective of the barroom as if it were his own.

Thorpe turned back to Longarm. "Now, what about you, sir? Do you need any medical attention?"

Longarm shook his head. "No, I reckon I'm fine. Ribs may be a little sore tomorrow, but I'll live."

"And you, Cappy?" Thorpe asked the old man. "I heard on the street that you were involved in this."

"That big ox come after me," Cappy said, pointing a shaking finger at Larribee. "He was gonna shanghai me and put me on one o' your ships!"

Thorpe frowned and shook his head. "Not on my orders, he wasn't. You paid off your debt to me, Cappy, by working on those last two voyages. We're square."

"Maybe you ought to have a talk with the fella, if he works for you," Longarm suggested.

Thorpe's voice was hard as he nodded and said, "I intend to do just that. It may be time for Captain Larribee to look for other employment." He looked over at Sandra Nolan. "I should have taken your advice and never hired him in the first place, Sandy."

Longarm saw her lips tighten at the familiar way Thorpe addressed her. But she didn't say anything about it. Instead she said, "Ernie's going to have Larribee locked up for starting the fight."

Thorpe's gaze darted back over to the bartender. "Is that true, Ernie?"

"Well . . ." Ernie hedged. "I was sure thinking about it, but if you're going to pay for the damages, Mr. Thorpe, and if you'll keep him out of here in the future, I guess it won't be necessary."

"Thanks, Ernie. Although to tell you the truth, I'm tempted to let the marshal haul him off to jail and leave him there for a while. It might put some sense in that thick-skulled head of his."

Longarm doubted that. Larribee struck him as the sort who would be slow to learn anything that went against what he wanted.

Thorpe asked, "Can I buy you a drink, Mr. . . . ?"

"Long. Custis Long." He left it at that, again not mentioning that he was a deputy U.S. marshal. "And I'll pass on the drink."

"Well, I'm glad to meet you, Mr. Long. I just wish it was under better circumstances."

The city marshal and a couple of deputies came in then, and they hauled the groggy Larribee to his feet. After the situation had been explained and Ernie had declined to press charges, the local lawman said to Thorpe, "Better get Larribee out to sea where he can't hurt anything."

"That's just what I intend to do," Thorpe agreed.

He shook hands with Longarm again, tugged on the brim of his hat as he nodded to Sandra, and followed Larribee as the big man shambled out of the barroom. Longarm watched them go. Cappy Fitzgerald came up beside him and said, "Mr. Thorpe ain't a bad fella, but that Larribee oughta be locked up."

Longarm couldn't argue with that. His bones already ached from being caught in that terrible grip.

"Come on, Cappy," Sandra said as she took the old man's arm. "I'll buy you some supper."

The old-timer perked up. "Really? That's mighty nice o' you, Sandy."

She looked over at Longarm. "Would you care to join us, Mr. Long?"

He gestured at his shirt, which was soaked in the spilled Maryland rye. "That sounds mighty nice, Miss Nolan, if you'll give me a few minutes to change my shirt."

She smiled for the first time since he had known her, and that made her even prettier. "Of course. We don't mind waiting, do we, Cappy?"

"Nope."

"There's only one condition," she added to Longarm. "Don't call me Sandy."

He chuckled. "I wasn't intending to, ma'am . . . Not until I get to know you better, anyway."

Chapter 3

Sandra Nolan's ship was called the *Night Wind*. It was a three-masted clipper, the sort of ship that sailed the seven seas and opened up the entire world for trade as American and British shipping empires grew over the past forty or fifty years. Sandra's operation wasn't quite that ambitious, though.

"We sail between here and Vera Cruz," she explained as she and Longarm and Cappy Fitzgerald ate supper at a restaurant a couple of blocks from the Nueces Hotel. According to both Sandra and Cappy, the food here was much better than the fare in the hotel dining room.

Longarm had to admit that the grilled fish on his plate tasted just fine and didn't have too many bones in it. The hash-browned potatoes and corn on the cob were good, too.

"It's a steady trade," Sandra went on. "The profits aren't huge, but we get by. Sometimes we're able to make a run over to New Orleans, and that helps."

"I reckon most folks just expect to see a boat like that going to Europe or China or someplace," Longarm commented.

"It's a ship, not a boat. A boat is smaller, and it doesn't carry paying passengers or cargo."

Longarm nodded but didn't say anything. Clearly, Sandra was the sort of person who was particular about what things were called, including herself.

"The *Night Wind* sailed the seas, all right," she said, a trace of wistfulness in her voice. "When I was growing up, my father had a whole fleet of ships just like her, and they visited practically every seaport in the world at one time or another."

"What happened to them?" Longarm asked, ignoring the warning glance that Cappy Fitzgerald shot toward him.

Sandra's voice hardened. "He lost them, one by one, when his business went bad. Until finally there was nothing left but the *Night Wind*. I inherited it when he . . . died. It was the only ship he was able to save. I swore to myself that I'd keep it going for him."

"I'm sorry to hear that he's passed on."

She shook her head. "It's been a couple of years. It doesn't hurt as much as it used to."

"Do you have any other family?" Longarm asked.

"My mother lives in Dallas. She wants me to sell the ship and move up there with her."

"But you ain't interested in doing that, are you?" Longarm guessed.

"Not at all. I like what I'm doing." Her voice had that defiant edge to it again, as if she were daring anybody to disagree with her.

Longarm wasn't going to do that. Instead, he said, "Then you should stick with it."

Cappy snorted. "Ain't gonna be easy to do, what with all the trouble linin' up a crew."

"I'll get a crew," Sandra snapped. "Don't you worry about that."

"It's all the worryin' that folks are doin' about Bloody Tom Mahone," Cappy said. "That's what makes 'em not want to go to sea."

Longarm had no idea who Bloody Tom Mahone might be, but his instincts told him to pursue the subject. Anything that affected shipping in the Gulf of Mexico might be tied in with the sinking of the revenue cutter.

"Who's this Mahone fella?" he asked, trying to sound idly curious. "He can't be any worse than Larribee."

"Actually, he is," Sandra said. "Or *was,* I should say. Larribee has killed a few men in brawls. Bloody Tom Mahone murdered scores of people. That's how he got the name. He was a pirate."

Longarm frowned. "You mean like Jean Lafitte?"

"As a matter of fact, Mahone was around at the same time as Lafitte. They were rivals, I guess you'd say. But Lafitte was never as bloodthirsty as Mahone. He didn't kill wantonly, for the pleasure of it."

Longarm leaned forward over the restaurant table. "You're not saying that this Mahone is still sailing around, are you?"

Sandra shook her head. "Oh, no. He's been dead for sixty-five or seventy years."

"That's what they'd like you to believe," Cappy put in ominously.

"If he was still alive he'd be over a hundred years old!" Sandra exclaimed. "Bloody Tom Mahone isn't responsible for all those ships that have been sunk in the Gulf."

In a hushed voice, Cappy said, "Some folks say they've seen him, and seen his ship, too! With Bloody Tom standin' there on the bridge, big as life!"

Longarm made an effort to control his excitement. Luck had played into his hands. Clearly, something else was going on in the Gulf besides the sinking of the revenue cutter, and this mismatched pair knew something about it.

"You say that ships have been sinking?" he asked.

"Five in the past two months," Cappy said. "And that don't include a gov'ment cutter that went down mysterious-like."

There hadn't been anything in the report from the Department of the Treasury about other ships being sunk besides the revenue cutter. Someone in Washington had either overlooked that fact or else deemed it not worthy of being mentioned.

Longarm thought it was important. It seemed at least possible, if not likely, that whoever was responsible for the sinking of the other ships might be to blame for the revenue cutter going down, too.

"And more than once," Cappy went on, obviously relishing his role as storyteller, "folks have seen a ship flyin' the skull an' crossbones around the places where those ships sunk. A black-sailed brig she was, with a black-souled pirate walkin' her decks as cap'n!"

"Cappy, stop it," Sandra said sharply. Other people in the restaurant were beginning to look over at them. "You know that's not true."

"I know what people say they seen, and I know what it means, too. Bloody Tom Mahone is back!"

"That's nonsense." Sandra put her napkin on the table and angrily pushed back her chair. "And I'm not going to sit here and listen to it."

Longarm wanted to stop her from leaving. He enjoyed her company, and he wanted to learn more about the trouble out on the Gulf. But he didn't want to overplay his hand and appear too interested in the ships that had been sunk.

Sandra paused, her irritation at Cappy apparently forgotten as she looked across the room at a man who was making his way toward the table. He was middle-aged, with graying red hair and a square, brick red face. He wore a blue uniform and carried a sailor's cap in his hand.

"Captain Morton, what is it?" Sandra asked as the man came up to the table.

Morton nodded politely to her as he said, "Good evening, Miss Nolan. I'm afraid I, ah, have some bad news for you."

When he hesitated, Sandra said impatiently, "Well, what is it?"

Morton squared his shoulders in determination. "I

21

won't be able to make the next voyage, ma'am. I'm re-signing as captain of the *Night Wind*."

"Resigning!" Sandra exclaimed. "But you can't do that."

"I can and I am," Morton insisted. "My wife knows that a sailor's life is a dangerous one. She's prepared to accept the chance that a squall or a hidden reef might get me one of these days. But she says she won't let me go out to get murdered by Bloody Tom Mahone."

Cappy nodded solemnly. "There's many a sailor as feels the same way these days, sir."

Sandra glared at Morton and said, "We have a contract, Captain. You're duty bound to serve as the master of the *Night Wind*."

"Well, then, ma'am, you'll just have to take me to court." Morton was calm but stubborn. Longarm could tell that the man wasn't going to change his mind.

"Damn it!" Sandra said, the outburst drawing even more attention from the diners in the restaurant. "I've got cargo bound for Vera Cruz. How am I supposed to get it there without a captain?"

Morton shrugged helplessly and then put on his cap. "I'm sorry, Miss Nolan. I don't know what else to tell you." He turned and walked out of the restaurant, with Sandra glowering after him as he went.

"Now what am I going to do?" she muttered. "There aren't any other captains around here who don't have a ship already." She turned and looked at Longarm.

All he could do was shake his head in reply to her unasked question. "I'd give you a hand if I could, ma'am, but you could put everything I know about sailing in my hat and still pert near have room for my head."

"I know that, Mr. Long," she said with an exasperated sigh. She sank back down in her chair, evidently having forgotten that she was about to leave. "I'll figure out something. I always do."

She didn't sound too sure of that, Longarm thought. From what she had explained earlier, she had been struggling for two years to keep her father's legacy alive. Captain Morton's resignation might mark the end of that struggle.

After a few minutes, Sandra said, "I'm going back to the office."

"Might ought to go home and get some sleep," Cappy suggested. "Problems have a way of lookin' not quite so big once you've slept on 'em."

Sandra smiled faintly. "I think this problem is going to look just as big or bigger in the morning, Cappy." She got to her feet, leaned over, and planted a quick kiss on the old man's forehead. "Good night. Good night to you as well, Mr. Long."

Longarm wouldn't have minded getting one of those kisses from her, but since he hadn't known her long enough to bring up the possibility, he just smiled and nodded to her. "Good night, Miss Nolan. And good luck."

"Thanks," she said wryly. "I'll need it."

When she was gone, Cappy said, "I sure hate to see that gal strugglin' so. She's tried mighty hard to make a go o' things since her pappy died."

"Have you known her for a long time?"

"Used to bounce her on my knee when she weren't nothin' but a tadpole. I worked on Nolan ships for twenty years, off and on. It's only been in the last couple o' years that I started takin' berths with other lines, like Harrison Thorpe's."

"And that was to pay off a loan," Longarm said.

Cappy shrugged. "Times has been tough. I'm squared away now, though."

An idea occurred to Longarm. Sandra's problems weren't really any of his business, but he liked her and wouldn't want to see her lose her ship. "Why don't you sign on as captain of the *Night Wind*?"

Cappy's eyes widened in a stare. "Me?" He shook his head emphatically. "No, sir. I ain't a cap'n. I feel sorry for the gal, but she'll have to find somebody else to be the master o' that ship."

23

He didn't sound like he could be persuaded otherwise. "It was just a thought," Longarm said. He changed the subject. "Tell me more about Bloody Tom Mahone."

"Be glad to." Cappy licked his lips. "But I might be able to talk a mite better if my mouth wasn't so dry."

Longarm chuckled. "I'll buy you a drink. You want to go back down to the hotel bar?"

"Actually, I was thinkin' more of Miguel's."

Longarm got to his feet and dropped a greenback on the table to cover the cost of the meals. With a grin, he said, "Lead the way, old son."

Chapter 4

Miguel's Cantina was one of the red-roofed adobe buildings that faced the Gulf across Water Street, just south of
the docks and the warehouse district. Several horses and
a couple of wagons were tied at the hitchrail in front of
the building. If it hadn't been for the vast expanse of water
across the street, the place would have looked right at
home in some dusty West Texas cattle town.

It wasn't much different inside, either. The floor was
made of planks rather than hard-packed earth. A scarred
bar ran down the right side of the room. Tables were
scattered to the left. There was a small dance floor in the
rear, and beyond it a beaded curtain closed off the arched
entrance to a back room.

Close to a dozen men stood at the bar drinking, and
another dozen sat at the tables playing cards or dice. A
few cantina girls worked carrying drinks to the tables. The
patrons were about evenly split between Mexican farmers,
gringo cowboys, and sailors. They all seemed to be getting along fairly well.

Longarm figured that situation could change in a hurry,
though, if somebody happened to get a burr up his behind
about something.

Cappy led the way to the bar, finding an empty spot
for him and Longarm. "*Hola,* Miguel," he called to the

bartender, a Mexican who had to have some Irish blood in him, to judge by his red hair: *"Dos cervezas, por favor."*

Miguel drew the beers and shoved them across the bar. The glasses were fairly clean, Longarm saw to his surprise. And when he tasted the beer he found it cool and not too bitter.

"Let's go sit down," Cappy said, hefting his beer mug. He went past a poker game between a couple of cowboys and three sailors and sat down at a table in the corner. Longarm joined him.

"You were going to tell me about Bloody Tom Mahone," Longarm reminded the old-timer.

Cappy took another swallow of beer and licked foam from his beard and mustache. "That's right. Sandy told you about he sailed the Gulf round about the same time as ol' Jean Lafitte. Folks knew his name from Havana to Vera Cruz, and most of 'em shuddered and crossed themselves when they heard it. Some pirates, all they was interested in was the booty. They'd board a ship and loot it, but then they'd let it sail on. Some of 'em liked to put the crew and passengers ashore and steal the ship itself. Not Bloody Tom, though. He killed all the prisoners and either torched or scuttled the ships that he captured. The blood of hundreds of people was on his hands, and that's why they called him Bloody Tom."

"Seems like somebody would have tried to stop him," Longarm said.

"Oh, they did. The navies of the United States, England, and Spain all went after him. But none of 'em could ever catch him. That black-sailed brig o' his was just too fast, and he knew every hidin' place up and down the Gulf Coast, from Florida to Mexico. I reckon that was his downfall in the end."

Cappy drained the last of his beer from the mug and set the empty on the table with a thump. Longarm knew what that meant. He signaled to Miguel for another round, and a pretty young woman in a peasant blouse and red embroidered skirt brought over the drinks on a tray. She gave Longarm a smile and a toss of her long black hair, and he thought she put a little extra sway in her hips as she walked back to the bar.

"As I was sayin'," Cappy went on when he had wetted his whistle again, "Bloody Tom knew every little cove and inlet along the coast. That's how he found Laguna del Diablo and decided to stash his loot there."

"The Devil's Lagoon," Longarm said quietly. "Not a very cheerful name."

"I wouldn't know whether it fits or not. I never saw the place myself. It's been gone for a long time."

Longarm frowned. "Wait a minute. How does a whole blamed lagoon disappear?"

"Hurricane," Cappy said. "But we're gettin' a mite ahead of the story."

Longarm leaned back in his chair and drank some beer. "Sorry. Go ahead."

"Did I mention Bloody Tom's treasure?"

"You said he decided to stash his loot at Laguna del Diablo."

Cappy nodded. "And he had plenty o' loot, too, because he'd robbed and sunk a lot of ships. Some folks said it amounted to a king's ransom. He found a good place on shore and buried it all, figurin' he'd come back later and get it. That's the way the story goes, anyway. I wasn't there to know if it's true."

"But then the hurricane came along . . ." Longarm prodded.

"And it was one hell of a blow. Now, understand, that ain't really the ocean out there." Cappy waved a gnarled hand toward the front of the cantina and the water lapping at the beach across the street. "Most landlubbers think it is, but 'taint even the Gulf. That's Corpus Christi Bay. There are barrier islands between us and the Gulf, and I'm talkin' all the way down the coast from here to Mexico, the longest damn beachfront you ever did see. There's a wide stretch of water between Padre Island—that's the

27

longest one—and the mainland. They call that the Laguna Madre."

Longarm knew everything the old man was telling him, but he kept his mouth shut and listened. Cappy seemed to be enjoying himself, and it didn't cost anything except enough beer to keep the old man properly lubricated.

"As I was sayin' about the hurricane, it come roarin' out of the Gulf and hit the island, and that didn't even slow it down, it was that big of a blow. Just washed right over the island and the Laguna Madre and hit the mainland about thirty miles south o' here. Right about the spot where the Laguna del Diablo was. It was such a powerful storm it changed the whole coastline. When the wind finally stopped blowin' and the floodwaters went down a mite, that little lagoon was gone. All anybody could figure was that the hurricane washed up a heap o' sand and shells and filled it up."

"And Bloody Tom's treasure was washed away, too?"

Cappy shook his head and sighed. "Nobody knows what happened to all that loot. Gold most of it was, accordin' to the story, with some jewels mixed in. It was buried good, in heavy chests. Could be it's still there. But all the landmarks were gone, and Bloody Tom couldn't find it no more. He spent years lookin'."

"That must've made him pretty mad."

"He was crazy mad to start with," Cappy said. "Losin' that treasure just made him crazier. He didn't go on his raids no more. He just spent all his time lookin' for the vanished Laguna del Diablo and that fortune in gold."

"What happened to him?"

Cappy shrugged and shook his head again. "Nobody knows for sure. Most folks say his crew o' cutthroats got tired of lookin' for the treasure and mutinied. They say Bloody Tom had to walk his own plank. Either that, or he got his throat slashed and was tossed into the Gulf." The old-timer leaned forward and lowered his voice. "But there's some as claim that the rest o' the pirates just deserted ol' Tom and left him to wander up and down the coast, lookin' for his treasure. They say if you sail out on the Laguna Madre at night, you can sometimes see him on the beach. Some even say his crew finally came back to him, and so he has his ship again, but not his gold. And he'll never rest until he finds it."

Longarm half-expected Cappy to jump at him and yell "Boo!" Instead Cappy just sat back and guzzled down the rest of his beer. Then he wiped the back of his hand across his mouth and said, "Of course, that's just the way the story goes. Probably ain't a word o' truth in it."

"But you said people claim to have seen Bloody Tom's ship around those ships that were sunk," Longarm pointed out. "You even seemed to believe it yourself."

Cappy pushed his lips in and out for a moment and then said, "I ain't sayin' one way or t'other. But there's *somethin'* out there on the Gulf sinkin' ships, and it might as well be the ghost o' Bloody Tom Mahone as anything else."

Longarm didn't really believe in ghosts, although during a few of his adventures he had encountered such strange things that he had been tempted to give credence to a supernatural explanation. Not in this case, though. No spook could sink a U.S. revenue cutter, as well as a handful of other ships.

"You know," Cappy went on, "you ain't said what it is that brings you to Corpus Christi, Mr. Long. Are you here on business or pleasure?"

"Business," Longarm said. "But I hope it's a pleasant visit, too. I'm a cattle buyer." There were several large ranches along the coast south of Corpus Christi, so it was a plausible explanation.

Cappy didn't have a chance to ask any more questions, because at that moment a man perched on a stool at the edge of the dance floor and began to strum a guitar. The young woman who had brought over the drinks earlier stepped out onto the floor and started to dance.

Every eye in the place was drawn to her, and for good reason. She was beautiful, with hair the color of a raven's wing that hung most of the way down her back, and flashing dark eyes, full red lips, skin the color of honey, and a lushly curved body that would make a bishop sit up and take notice.

She was graceful, too, as she moved around the dance floor. Her arms twisted in sinuous motions, and her long hair floated out around her as she twirled from one side of the floor to the other. The neckline of her white blouse scooped low, revealing the upper half of her full breasts. The firm globes were topped with large, dark nipples that were visible through the fabric of the blouse.

Cappy let out a long sigh as he watched the girl dance. "She's enough to make a fella wish he was forty years younger, ain't she?" he said wistfully.

Longarm was still plenty young enough not only to appreciate the dancer's charms but to do something about it if the opportunity arose. He said, "What's her name?"

"Antonia Lopez."

The name suited her, Longarm thought. As he drank his beer and watched her dance, the job that had brought him here to Corpus Christi was pushed momentarily to the back of his mind, though he would never forget about it entirely until he had concluded the case successfully.

Some of the men in the cantina began to clap along with the music of the guitar, and one of the cowboys at the bar let out a whoop. He was a stocky man with curly red hair under a pushed-back Stetson. He watched Antonia with a broad grin on his face.

The redheaded cowboy wasn't the only one who was really concentrating on the young woman. One of the sailors who had been playing poker let his eyes sweep over her with undisguised lust. He put a hand on the table and started to get to his feet.

At the same time, the cowboy who was so fascinated with Antonia moved away from the bar.

Longarm saw what was developing and frowned. The cowboy and the sailor both headed toward Antonia, each obviously intent on joining her dance. The cowboy was a little closer.

"Uh-oh," Cappy said as he noticed what was going on, too. "That's Brick Dunn. Rides for Hiram Prescott. He's a real hell-raiser when he's of a mind to be."

The cowboy called Brick Dunn probably didn't intend to cause trouble. But his senses were so inflamed by Antonia's dance that he couldn't think straight. He rushed up to Antonia as she spun around and grabbed her as she turned to face him. She gasped in surprise as his arms closed around her.

"Dance with me a while, honey!" Dunn yelled.

Miguel came from behind the bar. He might have managed to get Dunn away from Antonia and off the dance floor without a fight breaking out if he could have gotten there first.

But the burly sailor reached the scene ahead of him, and the man's hand came down hard on Dunn's shoulder.

"Get your filthy, cow-stinkin' paws off of her!" the sailor shouted as he jerked Dunn back.

Dunn didn't waste any time. His fist was already streaking toward the sailor's jaw even as he was hauled around. The blow caught the sailor off-balance and knocked him back a step. He let go of Dunn's shoulder.

"That's Nick Cooley," Cappy said to Longarm. "A brawler from way back."

Cooley proved that by catching himself and snapping a punch to Dunn's face as the cowboy bored in, thinking he had the advantage. The hard fist rocked Dunn's head back. Outraged yells went up from the other cowboys in the cantina as they saw one of their own being struck. Curses came from the sailors as they lunged to their feet, prepared to defend their friend.

"Oh, Lordy," Cappy said. "All hell's gonna bust loose now."

Longarm figured the old-timer was right, and he hated to see a brawl break out. He didn't want to get involved

31

in it. He was still sore from the earlier tussle with Larribee.

But as the two opposing groups suddenly flowed toward each other and fists began to fly, one of the sailors glanced in Longarm's direction and saw the Stetson on the big lawman's head. He bellowed, "Damned cow nurse!" and then snatched up a chair and threw it as hard as he could at Longarm.

Chapter 5

Instinct took over and sent Longarm diving out of his seat. The chair thrown by the sailor went over his head and smashed into the wall. The shattered pieces fell around Longarm.

The sailor wasn't going to let it go at that. With his hands balled into fists and curses on his lips, he charged across the cantina, straight at the man he had picked for his opponent.

Longarm scrambled to his feet and snapped, "Cappy, get out of here!"

"Hell no!" the old-timer replied. "I ain't never run away from a good scrap!"

Howling in anger, the sailor threw a roundhouse right at Longarm's head. Longarm ducked under it and smacked a left into the man's midsection. Though muscular, the sailor's belly was considerably less strong than Mauler Larribee's. He grunted in pain and doubled over as Longarm's fist sunk into his body.

But that wasn't enough to knock the fight out of him. Since he was bent over anyway, he lowered his head a little more and drove forward, crashing into Longarm like a maddened bull. The collision forced Longarm backward. He slammed into the wall.

Battling like this was getting damned old, Longarm

33

thought as the pain in his already sore ribs flared up again. He hammered a fist against the sailor's ear and followed it with a hard shove that sent the man stumbling back. Longarm stepped forward quickly and swung a left and a right. Both of the punches landed solidly and jerked the sailor's head back and forth. The man's knees buckled.

"Look out!" Cappy yelled.

Somebody landed on Longarm's back. An arm looped around his neck and clamped down hard on his windpipe. Longarm reached up and clawed at the man who had tackled him, but he couldn't get a good enough grip to pull the man off his back. Nor did a backward thrust of his elbow do any good.

There was only one thing left to do. Longarm twisted around and threw himself backward, pushing hard with his feet as he did so. Both men landed on a table that crashed to pieces under them, but the other man was on the bottom and cushioned the impact for Longarm.

The arm around Longarm's throat slackened as the impact of the fall stunned the second sailor. Longarm tore loose from the man's grip and rolled to the side. As he came to his feet, he saw the man lying there in the wreckage of the table, half-conscious and moaning.

Hearing a rusty old voice spitting curses, Longarm turned to see Cappy being held from behind by one of the cowboys. The puncher's arms were around Cappy's middle, and he was holding the old man a few inches off the floor. Cappy swung his arms in futile punches at another cowboy who stood in front of him laughing, just out of reach.

Longarm tapped the second cowboy on the shoulder, and when the man turned toward him, the big lawman walloped him with a hard right.

"Hey!" yelled the cowboy holding Cappy. "You can't do that, you son of a bitch!" He tossed Cappy aside and lunged at Longarm, fists swinging.

Longarm blocked the first couple of punches, but they came in such a flurry that he couldn't stop all of them.

34

The cowboy connected a couple of times and sent Long-arm reeling backward, shaking his head in an attempt to clear away the cobwebs. The cowboy scooped up the leg from a broken table and lifted it above his head, poising the makeshift club there as he lined up what might have been a skull-crushing blow if it had fallen.

It never fell, because at that instant, Cappy crashed an empty beer mug on the back of the cowboy's head. The table leg slipped from suddenly nerveless fingers and clat-tered to the floor. The cowboy followed it, landing in a senseless heap.

Longarm put a hand against the wall to steady himself. "Much obliged," he muttered to Cappy.

The old sea dog cackled. "I knocked the stuffin' outta that one, didn't I?"

"Yeah, you did," Longarm said. He grabbed his hat from the floor and then took hold of Cappy's arm. "Let's get out of here while we can."

The fight was still going on as knots of cursing, kick-ing, punching men moved back and forth on the dance floor and amid the wreckage of the tables. Miguel had retreated behind the bar and cast an occasional nervous glance over the top of the hardwood. Otherwise he stayed down and out of harm's way.

From what Longarm had heard, the cantina was the scene of such ruckuses on a fairly regular basis. Miguel was probably used to it by now and would wait it out, collecting money to pay for the damages once everybody was too tired to fight anymore.

Tugging Cappy with him, Longarm went toward the entrance and stepped out into the warm night. The breeze from the Gulf had died down, but it was still a pleasant evening. Longarm drew a deep breath of the salt-laden air into his lungs.

"By the great horn spoon!" Cappy said as they started down the street, straightening their disheveled clothes. "I was afraid trouble'd break out between those salts and

35

Prescott's boys, and sure enough, it did! Sort o' fun while it lasted, though."

"Prescott's one of the ranchers with a spread south of here along the coast?" Even as battered as he was, Longarm didn't forget about his job for very long. He wanted to learn as much as he could about the situation around Corpus Christi. A lawman never knew what might be important.

"Yep. Hiram Prescott come to Texas after the war, like so many others. He was a Yankee, though, not one o' the Rebs who drifted over here after they lost everything back home. Was you in the war?"

"Yeah, but don't ask me on which side," Longarm said. "That was a long time ago, and I disremember."

"I reckon I know what you mean. No point in holdin' old grudges." Cappy stuck his hands in his trouser pockets as he strolled along the street with Longarm. "Anyway, Cap'n King and ol' Mifflin Kenedy were already here, but Prescott gobbled up most o' the grazin' land that was left. He's built a good spread out of it and made a heap o' money, but folks don't like him much. They think he's too uppity, and too quick to step on anybody smaller who gets in his way."

That sounded like a lot of cattle barons Longarm had run into in various places across the West, and not surprisingly, things weren't too different here in the Coastal Bend of Texas. Still, he doubted that Hiram Prescott had anything to do with the ships being sunk in the Gulf. The rancher would be concerned only with what happened on land.

Longarm's steps had taken him back toward the Nueces Hotel, but he and Cappy hadn't reached it yet. He didn't know where Cappy lived, but the old man had to have someplace to stay. Longarm was about to suggest that they have one last drink in the hotel bar, when a sharp cry from out of the darkness made him stiffen in alarm.

That was a woman's voice, Longarm realized. He looked in the direction the cry had come from and saw

36

two figures struggling just inside the mouth of a shadowy alley.

"Stop fightin' and come on, you damn little hellcat!" a man grated. "You'll enjoy it, I guarantee!"

Instead of cooperating, the woman suddenly clawed at the man's face. When he cried out in pain and lurched back, she broke away from him and ran toward the street.

The man cursed and came after her, but he stopped short when Longarm stepped forward, palming the Colt from the crossdraw rig as he did so.

Corpus Christi had a few gas street lamps scattered along its downtown avenues. As the man and the woman came into the light from a lamp down the block, Longarm recognized both of them. The woman was Antonia Lopez, the serving girl and dancer from Miguel's Cantina. The man who was after her was Brick Dunn, the redheaded cowboy who rode for Hiram Prescott—and the man who had started the brawl in the cantina.

It was easy enough to figure out what had happened, and Longarm did so in a matter of instants. During the confusion of the fight, Antonia had slipped out of the cantina. Dunn had seen her leaving and come after her, preferring to pursue the girl rather than stay there and trade punches.

He had caught up with her and tried to drag her into the alley, and in the end he might have succeeded. But now he found himself staring down the barrel of Longarm's .45.

"I'd stop right there if I was you, old son," Longarm said in a low, dangerous voice.

"Who in blazes are you?" Dunn demanded angrily.

"Somebody who doesn't like to see a woman mistreated."

Dunn gave an ugly laugh. "I don't aim to mistreat her. I figure on treatin' her real nice, if you get my drift. Maybe a couple o' times."

Cappy had caught Antonia and stopped her blind flight. She shivered a little as he held her and patted her back

37

comfortingly. As Dunn made his crude comment, she turned her head to glare at him. *"Puerco!"* she spat.

Dunn shook with anger and stepped forward, even under the threat of Longarm's gun. "You can't call me a pig and get away with it, you whore!"

"That's enough, damn it," Longarm said. Chances were, Antonia *was* a whore, but that didn't give Dunn any right to call her one. "You better get out of here while you still can, mister."

Dunn sneered at him. "What are you goin' to do, gun me down in cold blood?"

"No, I'll just put a slug in your knee so it'll be stiff for the rest of your life and you won't ever be able to ride a horse again," Longarm said coldly. "Is that what you want?"

Dunn glowered at him in silence for a moment, then said, "I won't forget about this, mister. You stuck your nose into somethin' that wasn't none of your business, and sooner or later I'll even the score with you."

"I'll be waiting," Longarm said, "but you'll have to forgive me if I don't lose any sleep worrying about it."

Dunn muttered a few more curses and turned to stalk off down the street. Longarm kept an eye on him and didn't lower the Colt right away, just in case Dunn had some idea about spinning around and reaching for the iron on his hip. The cowboy kept going, though, and soon disappeared in the darkness.

"Gracias, señor," Antonia said to Longarm as he holstered his gun. "That man is a bad one. He would have hurt me if you and *Tio* Cappy had not come along when you did."

"You two know each other?" Longarm asked with a grin. Cappy still had his arms around Antonia and wore a blissful smile on his face.

She looked at the old-timer, laughed, and pushed away from him. *"Sí,* everyone in Corpus knows this old, how you say, sea dog."

"That's me, all right," Cappy replied with a grin. "And

when I'm around you, gal, you make me want to howl at the moon."

She laughed at him again, then turned to Longarm. "I am Antonia Lopez," she said as she held out her hand.

"Custis Long," he introduced himself. Her hand was smooth and warm and strong. He enjoyed holding it and maybe didn't let go quite as quick as he might have.

"I think Señor Brick is gone," she went on, "but just in case he hides in the night and tries to come after me again, will you take me home, Señor Long?"

"It would be my pleasure," Longarm assured her.

"How about me?" Cappy asked. "You want me to come along, too?"

"I reckon we can manage by ourselves."

"But you just got into town today," Cappy protested. "How'll you find your way back to the hotel?"

"I got a good sense of direction."

Antonia laid a hand on the old-timer's arm. "Thank you for your concern, *tio*. I am sure Señor Long will be able to return to his hotel . . . if he wishes to do so."

The undisguised invitation in her voice made Cappy mutter even more in jealousy. "Lord, I wish I was fifty again," he said as Longarm and Antonia started off, arm in arm. "Hell, I'd settle for sixty!"

Chapter 6

Antonia led Longarm to a small but neat adobe cottage on the northeast side of town where Corpus Christi Bay curved farther inland and became Nueces Bay, at the mouth of the Nueces River. As they paused on the tiny porch, she pointed toward a dark mass of land on the far side of the bay and said, "That is Indian Point. I grew up over there."

"So you've been around these parts all your life?"

"*Sí.*"

He thought about asking her if she knew anything about Bloody Tom Mahone, or about the ships that had been sunk out in the Gulf, but somehow this didn't seem like the right time.

Antonia leaned against him, and he felt her warm breath on his mouth as she came up on her toes and planted a quick kiss on him. "*Gracias,*" she whispered. "I am perhaps not an innocent, but I like to choose my own men."

"I'm glad I could help out," Longarm said as he slid his arms around her waist. She didn't try to pull away from him. Indeed, she pressed herself even closer to him without any urging. He brought his mouth down on hers.

Her lips parted, and her tongue eagerly sought his. Longarm felt a hardening in his groin as Antonia's breasts molded against his broad chest. She twined her arms around his neck. His hands moved down over the embroidered skirt to cup the exquisite roundness of her rump.

The heated, passionate kiss lasted a long time, and when it was finally over, Longarm said in a quiet voice, "I know you're grateful for the help, Antonia, but if all you're trying to do is say *gracias,* you've done that. I can go on back to the hotel now."

Of course, he would be mighty frustrated if he did, he added silently, but his conscience wasn't going to be satisfied unless he made the offer. Being a gentleman could be damned inconvenient sometimes, but he reckoned he was stuck with it.

Antonia gave a low, throaty laugh. "Go back to the hotel? Are you mad, Señor Long? I knew as soon as I saw you in Miguel's that I wanted you."

"You better call me Custis, then," he murmured just before he kissed her again.

Somehow, they wound up inside the cottage, in the small but clean bedroom. Antonia lit a candle, made sure the curtains were closed on the single window, and drew down the covers on the bed. As she turned back to Longarm, she pushed her low-cut blouse off her shoulders. The garment dropped around her waist, revealing her bare breasts.

They were lovely: firm round globes that rode high and proud on her chest, the pebbled nipples erect with longing. She cupped them and smiled at him in invitation. Longarm leaned closer to her and drew the left nipple into his mouth. His tongue swirled around it, making it harden and stand out even more. His teeth nipped it gently. Antonia giggled and then sighed with pleasure as he moved over to her other breast to repeat the sensuous process.

While he was licking and sucking her nipples, she pushed the blouse and her skirt down over her hips so that they fell to the floor. She wore nothing underneath them, so when she stepped out of them she was nude except for the soft slippers on her feet.

41

Longarm caressed her flanks, stroked her hips, and then lightly massaged her thighs. Her legs parted. He ran his fingers through the thick bush of dark hair over her groin and delved lower until he found the slick lips of her core. He slid a finger inside her.

She gave a little cry at this intimate caress. Tugging on Longarm's shoulders she urged him back to his feet and reached for the buttons of his vest. "You have on too many clothes," she said, her voice trembling a little with the urgency of her need.

Longarm couldn't have agreed more. He helped her undress him, and a few moments later he was as naked as she was, with his massive pole of male flesh jutting out from his groin. Antonia tried to wrap both hands around his shaft and murmured, *"Dios mío!"* when she failed. She looked up at him with a mixture of nervousness and anticipation.

"Don't worry," he assured her. "We'll work at it until it fits."

A smile spread across her face. *"Sí.* And I know just the way to start."

She had him lie down on the bed and then straddled his chest, facing away from him. As she lowered her head over his groin, her nether regions opened up to him. He saw the wet slit nestled in the thicket of fine-spun hair, topped by the puckered brown ring in the middle of the crease between her rounded cheeks. He eased a finger into that tight hole as his tongue began to glide along the fleshy folds of her gash.

She cried out softly, but she wasn't so distracted by what he was doing to her that she forgot about her plans for him. She grasped his shaft with both hands again and stroked the velvety head against her face, moaning a little as she nuzzled against the thick pole. She slid one hand all the way down it and cupped the heavy sacs at the base. Using the other hand to steady it, she began to lick around the crown.

The wet heat of her tongue made Longarm's hips lurch

a little. He wanted to thrust up into her mouth, but he forced himself to wait. She would get around to that in her own good time, he thought. He just hoped she wouldn't delay too long.

In the meantime he plugged his finger deeper into her back door and used his thumbs to spread her lips open even more. His tongue spread into her molten center. A heavy, fragrant dew flowed from her, making her even wetter than before.

She spread her mouth open wide and closed it over the head of his organ. Gradually, she swallowed even more of the pole. She was sort of a petite girl, and she could take only a few inches. But she made the most of them, sucking with abandon.

Just when Longarm thought his seed was going to explode down her throat, she lifted her head and gasped for breath. He slipped his finger out of her, sensing what was about to happen.

She swung around quickly and poised herself over his hips. She grasped him and guided him into her as she sat down hard and fast, filling herself with his maleness. She was so drenched that he went into her with ease. Her sheath stretched around him, and the head of his shaft hit bottom deep inside her. She was as full as she could possibly be, the wiry hair of her pubes mingling with his, the cheeks of her ass resting on his balls.

She put her hands on his chest to brace herself as she gasped and gave little mewling cries. They were both still, reveling in the exquisite sensation of being merged so closely together.

Longarm finally lifted his hands to her breasts, cupping them and thumbing her hard nipples. He raised his hips just a little. She pumped hers in response. His shaft slid back and forth in the superheated cavern of her femininity. She began to move faster and so did he. Within moments, he was plunging in and out of her in strong thrusts, and she matched him motion for motion. He felt the incredible strength of her femaleness clutching at him, milking the

43

essence out of him. Both of them were soaked in the juices of their passion.

And they were about to get even wetter, Longarm thought as he felt his climax boiling up. He couldn't stop it, didn't even try to. He might as well have tried to hold back the raging waves of the ocean. He moved his hands to her hips and gripped her tightly, jamming her down onto him as he drove upward. She cried out as he began to spasm. Her own culmination shuddered through her.

Longarm emptied his seed into her in spurt after white-hot spurt. The explosions shook him to his very center and seemed to go on forever.

But they finally ended and he sagged back on the bed, his pulse hammering inside his head, his body covered with a sheen of sweat, and his chest rising and falling strongly as he tried to catch his breath. Antonia collapsed on top of him, equally exhausted by the depth of the passion she had just experienced. Longarm could feel her heart beating strongly as she lay huddled on his chest.

"*Dios mío,*" she whispered at last. "Custis, you are *un hombre magnifico.*"

Longarm chuckled. "I've always figured that a fella's only as good at this as the gal he's with."

She lifted her head and kissed him. "You are so sweet. You will stay the night here." Her tone said that she wouldn't put up with any argument. "You will not go back to that hotel."

"No," Longarm agreed. "I won't."

They made love again before they dozed off, long after midnight. Then, the next morning, Longarm woke up with Antonia's tongue sliding up and down his erect manhood. When he was thoroughly aroused, she knelt on the edge of the bed with her lush backside in the air and begged him to take her from behind.

Longarm was glad to oblige.

It was almost an embarrassment of riches that later on she made him breakfast. She heaped his plate with tortillas and eggs and thick slices of ham. He ate heartily, washing down the food with swallows of strong coffee sweetened with chocolate. By the time Longarm was finished with the meal, he had recovered his strength and was ready to get back to work.

Antonia had grown up in the area and now worked in the cantina on the waterfront. She was bound to know something about the mysterious tragedies that had taken place in the past couple of months. Longarm said, "I'll bet you've known old Cappy for a long time."

"Ever since I was a little girl," she said as she lingered over her own coffee. "My father was a fisherman. I knew all the sailors."

Longarm was struck by the similarities between Antonia and Sandra Nolan. Both young women had grown up around the sea and sailors. But that was where it ended. Before her father's business reverses, Sandra had lived a life of comparative wealth and ease. Antonia and her family had probably scraped by. The experience certainly hadn't embittered her, though. This morning, after a night's sleep and with the war paint scrubbed off her face, she looked remarkably fresh and beautiful. Despite what she had said the night before, there *was* a certain innocence about her.

"You must have heard all the stories about Bloody Tom Mahone, then," he said.

She frowned. "The old pirate? *Sí,* I have heard of him."

"Cappy was telling me about some rumors that are going around. Some folks say that Bloody Tom Mahone is back, or at least that his ghost is responsible for sinking some ships out in the Gulf."

Antonia's expression grew solemn. "I have heard this talk, too. It makes me glad I am not a sailor." A little shiver ran through her. "I do not think I would like to sail the seas. I would be afraid of seeing that pirate and his ship with the black sails."

"Do you know anybody who's ever seen it?"

She frowned. "Why are you asking these questions,

Custis? What have you to do with a pirate . . . or a pirate's ghost?"

"Nothing really," he said with a casual shake of his head. "I'm just interested in spooky old stories. Always did like to hear about ghosts and such."

"This is why you came to Corpus Christi? To look for the ghost of Bloody Tomas Mahone?"

Longarm fell back on the same story he had told Cappy Fitzgerald the night before. "Nope, I'm a cattle buyer. Came to talk to some of the stockmen in the area."

"Then you will visit Señor Hiram Prescott?"

"Probably," Longarm said, wondering exactly what Prescott had to do with anything he and Antonia had been discussing.

She drew a deep breath and glanced around, almost as if she were afraid someone would overhear what she was about to say, even though she was in her own house. "If you go to Señor Prescott's ranch, you might talk to my cousin Consuela. She works there as a maid, in the big ranch house. She has seen the black-sailed ship of Bloody Tomas Mahone."

That took Longarm by surprise, but it was welcome news. He had hoped to locate a witness who had seen the so-called pirate ship. Now one had fallen right into his lap.

"Where did she see it?"

"In a cove on Señor Prescott's ranch, south of here. She rode out there one night . . . with one of Señor Prescott's cowboys . . ." Antonia looked down at the table and actually blushed. "You understand, Custis."

He nodded. "Sure."

"While they were there, Consuela saw the ship sail into the cove."

"What about the puncher who was with her?"

Antonia shook her head. "Consuela tried to show him, of course, but it was a dark night. He never saw the ship. But she insisted that they leave, before the ghosts of Bloody Tomas and his men came after them. They rode back to the ranch house. That was the only time Consuela ever saw the ship. She will not return to that place. She says it is cursed and haunted."

"Maybe she's right," Longarm said. "I might want to take a look at it anyway, just to sort of satisfy my curiosity. Do you know how to get there?"

"*Sí*." Antonia gave him directions on how to find the Prescott ranch and how to locate the cove as well. She looked worried, though, and added, "I do not think it would be wise to go there, Custis."

"Well, I probably won't have time anyway," he said, passing it off in a breezy tone.

"And if you go to Señor Prescott's ranch, be watchful. Brick Dunn rides for him, and he will wish to take vengeance on you for interfering with him last night."

"I came mighty close to doing more than interfering. For a nickel, I'd have ventilated the son of a buck. Has he ever bothered you before?"

Antonia shrugged prettily. "He comes to Miguel's and watches me dance and sometimes makes crude comments. Even when he says nothing, I do not like the way I feel when he looks at me. He has made me dance with him, but that is all. I have never gone with him."

"If he wants another ruckus, I reckon he can have one. But I'll do my best to stay out of his way."

"I think you should, Custis. Señor Brick, he would kill you if he could."

"Well, now," Longarm said, "I just won't give him the chance."

Chapter 7

When folks thought of Texas and cattle empires, what usually came to mind were the big ranches up in the Panhandle and out in West Texas. But Longarm knew some of the largest ranches in the world were down here in South Texas, spread out along the coast of the Gulf of Mexico.

Captain Richard King had started it all back in the fifties by buying up an old Spanish land grant of seventy-five thousand acres and running cattle on it. The King Ranch had grown considerably since then, to the point that Captain King had sold off some of his land to Mifflin Kenedy. Other cattlemen, like John T. Wood and George W. Fulton, had moved into the area.

Longarm had seen Fulton's mansion, up the coast a ways in a little seaside settlement that bore the rancher's name. The huge house, equipped with expensive furniture and all the latest luxuries, wouldn't have been out of place in New York City or Philadelphia. Raising cattle was a big—and profitable—business in these parts.

The Prescott spread was the Diamond HP. The brand was burned into a long, thick plank that hung over the gate in the road that ran south from Corpus Christi. A barbed wire fence ran in either direction from the gate, as far as the eye could see. Of course, to the east it was only a few miles to the Gulf, but on this coastal plain the terrain was so flat the horizon seemed closer than it really was. That was why a fella could ride for hours and never seem to get anywhere.

Longarm had seen bloody wars fought over barbed wire. Evidently the devil's strands had been accepted down here. He unlatched the gate, swung it back, rode through, and closed it behind him. Then he followed the road south.

After leaving Antonia's cottage, he had gone to his room at the Nueces Hotel long enough to wash up and trade his brown tweed suit for denim trousers and a butternut bib-front shirt. Then he had rented a horse at a local livery stable and ridden out of Corpus Christi.

The countryside in these parts always reminded him of West Texas. There was more and greener vegetation, of course, but the flat, sandy ground and the low scrub brush that covered much of it looked about the same at first glance.

The biggest difference was that in this humidity, just moving around a little was enough to make somebody break a sweat. The dry air of West Texas sucked up perspiration just like it did all the other forms of moisture.

Longarm came to a smaller trail that angled to the east from the main road. According to what Antonia had told him, that trail led over to the coast. He turned his rented horse onto it. He wanted to have a talk with Hiram Prescott sooner or later, but for the time being he would avoid the ranch headquarters and take a *pasear* around by himself. He wanted to have a look at that cove where Antonia's cousin had seen the pirate ship.

After a half hour or so, he came to the water. He reminded himself that this wasn't the actual Gulf of Mexico but rather the Laguna Madre, as Cappy had said. It might as well have been the ocean, because Longarm couldn't see land on the other side of it, even though he knew Padre Island was out there somewhere. Ships could get in and out of the Laguna Madre through Mustang Pass, up close to Corpus Christi.

The grassland ran all the way to the edge of the water. The trail turned and meandered along the shore, following the ragged outline of the coast. Longarm rode along it, knowing he ought to reach the cove pretty soon. It was only a few miles south of the spot where the trail hit the coast, Antonia had told him.

Sure enough, he soon spotted water ahead of him, as well as to his left. The cove opened up before him. He reined in and studied it. The little bay was perhaps a quarter of a mile across and extended inland at least five hundred yards. It looked almost like the sea had taken a bite out of the mainland here.

Longarm turned his horse and started along the shoreline, intending to ride all the way around. To his left, the water washed up only a few feet from the edge of the trail. To his right was a salt marsh. The path was on slightly higher ground, but anytime the water got up a little, it would slosh over the trail and onto the lower ground beyond it. That was how the marsh had formed, Longarm guessed.

He hadn't seen a soul since he'd ridden onto the Diamond HP. The only other living things he had spotted were some longhorn cattle and a bunch of seagulls. He might as well have been alone here, as alone as the first Spanish explorers who had come to this seacoast hundreds of years earlier.

A second later, he knew that wasn't the case at all, because a rifle barked sharply and he heard the whip-crack of a bullet passing close beside his head.

The sound of the shot came from his right, inland. There was no cover along the trail, no trees close enough to reach before the bushwhacker could take another shot at him. He couldn't count on the rifleman missing twice.

Longarm went out of the saddle in a dive that took him to the right, into the edge of the salt marsh. He landed in the mud and rolled over, trying to keep his Colt out of the water. The grass was three or four feet tall around him, tall enough to hide him if he stayed low. He couldn't move around much, though, or the bushwhacker would be able to tell where he was by the way the grass was waving.

He heard the rattle of hoofbeats as his horse ran on down the trail, probably spooked by the shot. So now he was set afoot as well as pinned down by an unseen rifleman.

It was amazing how many things could go wrong in such a short period of time.

Crouched in the shallow, muddy water amid the reeds and the grass, he drew his gun and waited. It was possible the bushwhacker might have mistaken his dive for the sort of tumble that a wounded man took from a saddle. If the rifleman thought he was hit, then sooner or later the man would come to see for sure and find out if he was dead. That was just human nature.

So all he had to do, Longarm thought, was to stay still and let the would-be killer come to him.

The minutes passed with agonizing slowness. The hoofbeats of Longarm's horse had faded away. When he finally heard a horse approaching on the trail, he was pretty sure it wasn't his mount returning. In all likelihood, this animal belonged to the bushwhacker.

The smell of saltwater and rotting vegetation filled Longarm's nostrils. He was wet, muddy, and miserable, and he wanted out of this marsh. He was angry, too, that someone had taken that shot at him. He wanted to lunge up out of the grass and have a showdown with the bushwhacker.

Instead he forced himself to be patient. The hoofbeats paused, then started again, and then paused for a second time very close to where he was hidden. He had a feeling the rifleman was looking for him, trying to figure out where he had gone into the marsh.

After a few moments, the horse moved on. That was what Longarm had been waiting for. Now the bushwhacker had gone past his position and probably had his back to him. Longarm could get the drop on him.

Clutching his revolver in his right hand, Longarm used his left to balance himself as he moved toward the edge of the marsh as quietly as possible. He didn't rush. He didn't want the bushwhacker to hear the grass rustling.

When he reached the edge of the growth, he looked out and saw the rider about forty feet away. The man was slender and rode a good-looking bay horse, and he had a Winchester in his hands, ready to fire as he rode slowly past the marsh, studying the grass.

Longarm straightened from his crouch, feeling cramped muscles protest as he did so. He leveled the Colt and called in a steady voice, "Hold it right there, old son!"

He saw the bushwhacker stiffen and start to turn in the saddle. If the rifle barrel came toward him, Longarm was going to fire. He would aim to wound, though. He didn't want to kill the bushwhacker. For one thing, he had too many questions to ask the man.

Like why in the world the son of a buck wanted him dead.

The man didn't bring the rifle around. He froze instead, obviously figuring out that Longarm had the drop on him. Longarm walked along the trail toward the rider, saltwater sluicing from his trousers and sloshing unpleasantly inside his boots.

"Throw down that Winchester," he called when he had halved the distance between himself and the bushwhacker. The man followed orders, tossing the rifle across the trail to the right.

But at the same instant, as Longarm's eyes involuntarily flicked to the right to follow the Winchester, the rider went out of the saddle to the left. Longarm fired, but the shot came a whisker of a second too late. The man moved with catlike quickness. He hit the trail on the far side of the horse, rolled over, and came up with a pistol in his hand.

The pistol cracked and sent a bullet whining past Longarm. He bit back a curse. The horse was in the way, and he couldn't get a clear shot at the man. There was still no place to find any cover out here, so he did the only thing he could.

He charged straight at the bushwhacker.

It was a dangerous move, no doubt about it. He had a little less than twenty feet to cover, running right toward the other man's gun. But the bay horse was skittish and started jumping around in the trail, and that gave Longarm all the distraction he needed. The bushwhacker got off another shot, but it didn't come anywhere close.

Then the horse bolted. The bushwhacker tried to grab the reins but missed. Longarm had a clear shot then, but he didn't take it. Instead he threw himself forward in a diving tackle.

He was considerably bigger than the bushwhacker, and the jarring impact of the collision sent the man flying backward. He landed on the trail with a pained grunt. The next instant, Longarm's weight smashed down on him.

The bushwhacker wasn't completely stunned, though. He lashed out at Longarm with the pistol, which he had managed to hang on to. The blow clipped Longarm on the side of the head, but there wasn't much power behind it. The pain was an annoyance more than anything else and made him angrier than he had been to start with.

He grabbed the wrist of the man's gun hand and twisted hard. Bones grated together under the pressure. The man yelped in pain and let go of the pistol. Longarm kept his hold on the man's wrist. It was entirely possible the bushwhacker might have another weapon on him, and Longarm didn't want to give him a chance to grab for it.

"You bastard!" the bushwhacker said. "Get *off* me!"

The words hit Longarm hard, because they were in a woman's voice. He was lying on top of the bushwhacker and hadn't noticed that the body under him was particularly womanly. It was more like a bundle of ropes and wires.

But when he looked, he saw that the bushwhacker's

hat had come off and let a mass of thick blond hair spill loosely from it. The jutting chin was smooth and beardless, and deep blue eyes peered out from behind long blond lashes. The bushwhacker was definitely a woman.

But considering that she had already taken several shots at him, Longarm kept her pinned to the ground for the time being.

"Who are you?" he demanded. "Why'd you try to kill me?"

"*Get off me!*" she repeated, ignoring his questions. She was starting to sound a little hysterical. She must have decided that he wasn't going to shoot her or hit her, because she continued to struggle and writhe around underneath him. She had no chance of getting loose, though. He weighed twice as much as she did and was a lot stronger.

That didn't stop her from fighting. Nor did it keep her from cursing him. She wore range clothes like a cowboy, and she must have been around enough punchers in her lifetime for her to have picked up a lot of their colorful obscenities. Now that he'd had a better look at her, Longarm decided that she was pretty . . . or at least she would have been if she hadn't been spitting cuss words at him.

He was holding her left arm down with his right arm. When he moved it to holster the Colt, her arm was free for a moment and she punched at him with a small fist. He grabbed that wrist, too, and managing to get his feet under him, he stood, hauling her upright with him. He towered over her.

She kicked at his shins, making him dance a little to avoid the toes of her boots. "Damn it, stop that!" he burst out. "I ain't gonna hurt you, unless you make me do it!"

Suddenly, she lifted a knee at his groin. He turned his hips just in time to take the blow on his thigh. That was it, he thought. He'd had just about enough of this hellcat.

He took hold of both of her wrists in his left hand. They were slender enough that that wasn't a problem.

Then he said, "For the last time, settle down, or I'll have to wallop you!"

She was still yelling and spitting and raising a ruckus, so he didn't hear the other horses right away. But as he drew back his right arm so that he could slap her if he had to, he heard the swift rataplan of hoofbeats, and then a second later a gun blasted. He twisted around, taking the girl with him, and reached for his gun.

"Freeze, mister!" a man called. "Let go of her right now, or by God, I'll put a bullet through your head!"

Chapter 8

The man who voiced the threat was in the forefront of a small group of riders who had just reined in about thirty feet away. They all looked like cowboys, and Longarm would have been willing to bet they were punchers who rode for Hiram Prescott's Diamond HP.

The spokesman cradled a rifle in his hands and had a bead drawn on Longarm. He seemed to be tall, though it was hard to tell with a man on horseback, and had a craggy, cold-eyed face under a broad-brimmed black hat. Longarm didn't doubt that he would make good on his threat.

"Shoot him, Chuck!" the young woman urged. "Shoot the son of a bitch!"

"Better hold up a minute," Longarm said, keeping his voice calm and level. He noticed that a couple of the cowboys were leading riderless horses and recognized the animals as his rented mount from Corpus Christi and the big bay that the young woman had been riding. "Best to eat an apple one bite at a time, I always say."

"I don't give a damn about any apples," the man with the rifle said. "Who are you, mister, and why were you attacking Miss Prescott?"

Longarm glanced at the young woman. "Any relation to Hiram Prescott?" he asked.

"He's my father," she said, "and if I ask him, he'll have you strung up by your toes, you damned—"

"No need for that, Judith. Just step away from the fella. He'll let go of you . . . if he wants to keep on living, that is."

She did as the man with the rifle told her. Longarm released his grip on her wrists, and she moved away from him. But not before looking like she wanted to either slap him silly, claw his eyes out, or both. She was a gal who definitely had a problem with her temper, Longarm thought.

The man called Chuck finally lowered his Winchester, but he kept it pointing in Longarm's general direction. Several of the other men had revolvers in their hands, too. Longarm was too outnumbered to do anything except co-operate.

"Now," Chuck said, "I want some answers to my questions, mister."

Longarm had to think for a second to remember what those questions had been. Then he said, "My name is Long, and I wasn't attacking Miss Prescott."

"That's a lie!" she said. "He knocked me down, and he jumped on top of me and wouldn't get off! He was trying to force himself on me!"

Chuck glared at Longarm. "A man who'd do something like that ought to be strung up."

"Wasn't the way it happened," Longarm said with a shake of his head. He pointed to the two guns lying in the trail. "There's her rifle and pistol. Check 'em both and you'll see that they been fired recent-like."

"What about your gun?" Judith Prescott said. "It's been fired, too, because you shot back at me!"

She tried to stop short, but the words were already out. Longarm wasn't sure the admission would make any difference, though. This was her father's ranch, and he was a stranger. She could claim just about anything she wanted to and be believed.

Still, he had to try to get through to Chuck. Longarm

was just glad that Brick Dunn wasn't among this group of Diamond HP hands. Dunn probably would have shot him without any hesitation.

"I told you my name is Long. I'm a cattle buyer. I just rode out here to see Mr. Prescott. That's all. The young lady took a shot at me. I admit I tried to stop her from doing it again. But I didn't know she was a woman when I jumped her. Dressed like she is, with her hair up under her hat, I thought she was a fella."

"Well!" Judith sniffed. "You don't have to be insulting."

Chuck didn't look convinced. "If you came to see Mr. Prescott, what're you doing over here by the water? The ranch house is a good four or five miles west of here."

"Reckon I took a wrong turn in the trail," Longarm said with a shrug.

If it came down to it, he would pull out the leather folder he carried in his pocket. It contained his badge and bona fides. The fact that he was a deputy United States marshal would probably carry enough weight so that Chuck wouldn't shoot him out of hand.

Longarm didn't want to reveal that unless he had to, though. He often had more success conducting an investigation when folks didn't know who he really was.

Finally, Chuck shoved his Winchester back in the saddle boot and motioned for the other men to put up their guns. "I reckon there's some truth to your story, mister," he said. "We heard several shots, and then we found your horse and Judith's coming along the trail. Figured there was some trouble."

"Trouble!" Judith exclaimed. "Of course there was trouble! I told you what happened. Aren't you going to shoot him, or hang him, or something?"

"Only if your pa tells us to." Chuck walked his horse closer to Longarm. "I'll take your gun, Long."

Under the circumstances, Longarm decided it would be safe enough to hand over the Colt, although he didn't like to be without an iron. He suspected that Chuck would take him to the ranch headquarters and turn the matter over to Hiram Prescott. Longarm wanted to talk to the rancher anyway.

But his look at the cove where Bloody Tom Mahone's ship had been seen sure hadn't paid any dividends. He hadn't learned a damned thing about the case, and he doubted that Chuck and the other cowboys were in much of a mood to answer questions about a black-sailed ship and the ghost of a long-dead pirate.

Judith Prescott certainly wasn't. She was still glaring daggers at him. As she took the reins of her horse from the man who had been holding them and swung up into the saddle, she said, "I still think he's one of those damned rustlers. That's the only reason I took a shot at him in the first place."

Longarm hadn't heard anything about any rustling going on around here, but he had arrived in the Corpus Christi area less than twenty-four hours earlier, as difficult as that was to believe considering everything that had happened.

He stepped up into his own saddle and said, "Having trouble with wideloopers, are you?"

Judith gave a contemptuous, unladylike snort. "You know good and well we are, because you're part of the gang!"

She had accused him of being a rapist and now a rustler. Longarm wondered what was going to be next.

"Sorry to disappoint you, ma'am, but like I said, I'm here to *buy* cattle, not to steal them."

Judith sniffed in disbelief and yanked her horse's head around. She clapped her spurs to the animal's flanks and sent it lunging into a gallop that carried her on down the trail ahead of the rest of the group.

One of the Diamond HP punchers had removed Longarm's Winchester from the saddle boot, so now he was unarmed except for the little .41 caliber, over-and-under derringer which was welded to the other end of the chain attached to his pocket watch. Outnumbered as he was, though, that derringer wouldn't do him much good in a fight, so he continued to cooperate, riding with the cowboys toward the ranch headquarters.

"My name's Chuck Ballinger," the group's spokesman introduced himself. "I'm the foreman of Mr. Prescott's crew."

"Custis Long is the full handle. I'd say that I'm pleased to meet you, Chuck, but I reckon I'll reserve judgment on that."

The foreman laughed. "That's probably a good idea, because if you *do* turn out to be a rustler, chances are you'll wind up dancing on air. The old man likes to take care of problems like that himself, instead of turning them over to the law. And there's a bunch of big live oak trees all around to the house."

"For the time being, why don't we assume that I'm telling the truth and that I'm not a rustler," Longarm suggested. "Tell me about the troubles you've been having."

Ballinger shrugged. "Same old story that's happened again and again, any place there are cattle. Somebody's been stealing them. Never more than a few hundred head at a time, but it adds up when it happens a couple of times a week for several months."

"Have you tried trailing the thieves?"

"Of course we have," Ballinger said in a slightly impatient tone. "The trail always runs out when the stolen cows get to the water."

Longarm looked over at him. "You mean they're taking the rustled stock off by ship?"

"That's all we can figure. There are a bunch of coves up and down this coast like that one where we found you and Miss Prescott. The wideloopers drive the cattle over to one of the coves, where a ship's waiting to pick them up."

"Seems like you could put a stop to it by riding patrol on the coast," Longarm said.

"You'd think so, but those bastards are slick. They manage to be where we ain't. And there's just too much coastline for us to cover all of it, all the time."

That comment put an idea in Longarm's head. It would be easier for the rustlers to operate and to get away with their stolen stock if they had someone on the inside at the Diamond HP, tipping them off about which areas of the coast would be the safest.

That same thought had probably already occurred to Ballinger, so Longarm didn't say anything about it. No doubt the foreman was already trying to root out the traitor, if there was one.

Longarm looked along the trail ahead of them. Judith Prescott was almost out of sight, still riding hard. "That gal's sure got a temper," he said.

"Watch your mouth, mister," Ballinger snapped, his affable manner hardening. "I won't listen to any bad talk about the boss's daughter."

Was it the fact that Judith was Hiram Prescott's daughter that made Ballinger defensive about her? Longarm wondered. Or did Ballinger have a soft spot for her because he was attracted to her?

Longarm didn't know, and although he thought Judith was good-looking in a tomboyish way, he didn't find her arrogance and belligerence the least bit appealing. Maybe Ballinger saw something in her that he didn't.

Like the fact that she might inherit one of the biggest ranches in Texas . . . ?

Longarm put all that speculation out of his head for now. It didn't have anything to do with why he was here.

He wondered, though, if the rustling that plagued the Diamond HP might be connected with the sunken ships and the rumors of Bloody Tom Mahone's return. If fear of the pirate meant fewer ships sailing in the Gulf, wouldn't that make it easier for the rustlers' ship to carry away the stolen cattle?

Longarm thought he might be on to something, but at the same time, he knew he was still a long way from being able to see the whole picture. At this point, any theory he came up with was little more than sheer speculation.

After riding on in silence for a while, they came within sight of a clump of trees. As they approached, Longarm spotted buildings among the trees and knew they were getting close to the ranch headquarters. He saw barns and corrals, and in the middle of the thick-trunked live oaks with their spreading canopies sat a whitewashed, two-story house with several gables. It was a nice-looking place, and well cared for.

Judith had reached home quite a while before the rest of the group, and there was no telling what sort of yarn she had spun about what happened. Longarm had a suspicion that she had colored the facts a mite, though, when a middle-aged man with white hair and a ruddy face stepped onto the porch with a shotgun in his hands. As the riders reined to a stop in front of the house, the man lifted the greener, pointed it at Longarm, and shouted, "Get out of the way, boys! I'll teach this son of a bitch to lay his dirty hands on my girl!"

Chapter 9

Longarm felt a coldness in his belly and along his spine as he found himself staring down the twin barrels of the scattergun. The man who trained the weapon on him had to be Hiram Prescott, and from the looks of it, the rancher was ready to blast Longarm as soon as his men got out of the line of fire.

"Hold on, Boss," Chuck Ballinger said hurriedly. "You don't want to do that."

"Why the hell not?" Prescott demanded. "He tried to molest Judith, didn't he?"

"Maybe not. From what he said, she tried to kill him, and he was just defending himself."

Prescott snorted. "A likely story! Now get out of the way, damn it, so I can shoot him!"

Longarm saw where Judith Prescott got her temper and her high-handed ways. She was the apple of her daddy's eye, and she hadn't fallen very far from the tree.

Ballinger edged his horse over so that he was between Longarm and Prescott. "I reckon you'd better listen to him, Mr. Prescott," the foreman said. "He claims he's a cattle buyer who rode out here to see you. If that's true, you don't want to kill him."

"If it was true, what was he doing over by the water?"

Prescott didn't lower the shotgun. "I think he's one of the rustlers, scouting us for their next raid."

Longarm was getting sick and tired of this. He never liked to have guns pointed at him, especially greeners that could blow him apart with their double load of buckshot. He was about to tell Prescott that he was threatening a federal lawman, when a harsh, angry voice called, "What the hell is *he* doing out here?"

Longarm's jaw tightened as he saw Brick Dunn striding toward them from a long, low building that was probably the bunkhouse. The redheaded puncher's face was twisted in angry lines. As bad as it had been, the situation had just taken a turn for the worse.

Prescott said, "You know this man, Brick?"

"Damn right I do," Dunn answered. "He's the fella who started that brawl in Miguel's last night and then later tried to shoot me."

Was *everybody* on this ranch full of lies? Longarm thought angrily.

"That's not the way it was," he said, making an effort not to fly off the handle. Maybe being hot-tempered was contagious. He looked around at the other cowboys and went on, "Some of you were probably in the cantina last night. You know I didn't start that fight."

He didn't add that Dunn had been responsible for that, with his drunken pawing of Antonia.

One of the punchers drawled, "I was there, but I don't rightly recollect who threw the first punch. Now that I think about it, though, I'm pretty sure this fella was in the middle of it, Boss. I saw him tusslin' with a couple of our riders."

Longarm couldn't deny that. He had fought with both cowboys and sailors during the melee.

Prescott glowered at him. "What is it with you, mister? You got a grudge against this ranch, or just cattlemen in general?"

"I don't have a grudge against anybody," Longarm said with a sigh of frustration. "I don't deny that I was at

Miguel's last night, but I didn't start the fight. And I didn't take a shot at Dunn there."

"You pulled a gun on me!" Dunn accused.

"But I never fired it. And I wouldn't have pulled iron in the first place if you hadn't been bothering that gal."

Dunn sneered at him. "There's proof right there you're a liar, mister. Nobody would have to fight with that little Mex whore to get her to go with them. She belongs to anybody with four bits in his pocket."

"That's not what she told me, old son," Longarm returned coldly. "I reckon there ain't enough money in the world to get her to put up with the likes of you."

He knew he was asking for more trouble by prodding Dunn, but he was sick and tired of the whole thing. Before Dunn could react, however, a new voice asked, "What whore are you talking about?"

"Judith!" Hiram Prescott roared. "Get back in the house, girl! This is no talk for a female to be listening to."

From the open doorway behind her father, Judith stepped onto the porch. "I know all about whores, Father," she said haughtily. "I even know what men do with them."

"Judith!"

She ignored Prescott's red-faced bluster and looked at Longarm. "I just thought you were a rustler. I didn't know you were a whoremonger, too."

Longarm remembered reading a story about a gal who fell down a rabbit hole and landed in a place where everybody was loco. He was beginning to wonder if the same thing had happened to him.

One of the other cowboys contributed a note of sanity by saying, "Uh, Boss, I think I saw this fella gettin' off the stage in Corpus yesterday. I ain't sure he's been around here long enough to be part of that gang of rustlers."

"He *did* say he was a cattle buyer," Ballinger put in.

"I tell you, he took a shot at me!" Dunn said.

"If you were associating with a whore, you probably deserved it, Brick," Judith Prescott said, a prim expression on her face. She pushed past her father and came down the steps to stand next to Longarm's horse. "Have I done you a great disservice, sir? Was I mistaken about why you were on the Diamond HP range?"

"Yes, ma'am, you were," Longarm told her. He wasn't sure he believed for a second that this sudden change in attitude on Judith's part was genuine, but if it was, he wanted to take advantage of it. "I'm sorry about knocking you down. No offense intended, but at the time I really did think you were a fella."

She laughed. "Of course you did. With me dressed like this, I can see why you made that mistake." She turned toward the porch. "Father, put that shotgun down! I was all wrong about Mr. . . . ?" She looked back over her shoulder at him.

"Long, ma'am. Custis Long."

"I'm pleased to meet you, Mr. Long. Now," and she turned back to Prescott, "I insist that we make Mr. Long welcome, Father. He's here to talk business."

Prescott frowned. "You don't want him killed anymore?"

"Not at all."

Brick Dunn said, "Damn it, I still got a score to settle with him!"

"Go back to the bunkhouse, Brick," Ballinger ordered. "I reckon this is over."

Longarm saw the murderous fury in Dunn's eyes and knew it wasn't over, but at least the showdown had been postponed again. As Dunn stomped off, muttering curses under his breath, Prescott finally lowered the barrels of the scattergun.

"Come on inside, Mr. Long," he said grudgingly. "I'm still not convinced you're what you claim to be, but I'm willing to talk about it." He patted the shotgun's stock. "But I'll have this greener handy, so don't get any ideas about trying anything funny."

"You don't have to worry about that, sir." Longarm swung down from the saddle and handed the horse's reins to one of the cowboys.

The house was opulently furnished, with thick rugs on the floors, overstuffed furniture, and silver and brass everywhere. Prescott led the way into a parlor, followed by Longarm, Judith, and Chuck Ballinger. The rancher said, "I suppose I ought to offer you a drink."

"It's a mite early for that, ain't it?"

Prescott snorted. "As those damned sailors say, the sun's already over the yardarm somewhere in the world."

"In that case, I'm much obliged, sir."

Prescott picked up a decanter from a heavy mahogany sideboard and poured brandy for himself, Longarm, and Ballinger. "Judith, go tell Consuela that we'll have a guest for dinner," he instructed.

Judith seemed reluctant to leave, but she did as her father told her. Longarm recalled that Consuela was Antonia's cousin and the one who supposedly had seen Bloody Tom Mahone's ship. He wanted to find a private moment to talk with the woman while he was here, if he possibly could.

"To your health, Mr. Long," Prescott said as he lifted his snifter of brandy. Now that he had gotten over his initial anger, he seemed determined to be a good host.

"And to yours, sir," Longarm replied. Ballinger didn't say anything, but he sipped the brandy when the others did.

Prescott licked his lips and said, "All right, what's all this about you being a cattle buyer?"

"I have contracts with some of the biggest packing houses in Chicago," Longarm lied easily. "If you want references, you can check with Miss Jessica Starbuck at the Circle Star Ranch out in West Texas. We've done business many times in the past."

Prescott nodded slowly. "Starbuck, eh?" Clearly, he had heard of the Circle Star and knew the respect that vast spread commanded.

Longarm smiled to himself. If Prescott sent off a wire to Jessie Starbuck, she would back up Longarm's story without hesitation. And it was certainly true that she and Longarm had worked together many times in the past . . . only they had been chasing down thieves and killers, not buying and selling cattle.

Warming to the story, he went on, "I've never had any dealings down here in South Texas, though, so I thought it might be worth a trip to see if I could expand my operation. From what I've seen so far, you've got a good-looking spread with a lot of fine cattle on it."

Prescott grunted. "There's a damn sight fewer of them than there used to be."

"Yeah, Chuck here told me you'd been losing stock. With a ranch this big, it seems like rustlers would have a hard time even making a dent in your herds."

Prescott tossed off the rest of his brandy and said, "That's where you'd be wrong. Of course, I still have a lot more stock than I've lost. It would take that gang several years to clean me out at the rate they're going. But if nobody puts a stop to what they're doing, who's to say they won't keep it up for years?"

He had a point there. A man could bleed to death from a small cut, and a ranch, even a big one, could be stripped of stock by a persistent gang of outlaws.

"We'll stop 'em before that happens, Mr. Prescott," Ballinger said. "You can count on that."

"You haven't had any luck so far," Prescott said curtly. "Those rustlers come and go like ghosts."

And there was his opening, Longarm thought. He said, "You mean like Bloody Tom Mahone?"

Prescott had picked up the decanter to pour more brandy into his glass. He stopped short at Longarm's words, and a few drops of the brandy spilled on the sideboard. Prescott set the snifter aside and said, "That's nonsense. And if you just got to Corpus Christi yesterday, how do you know about Mahone?"

"Quite a bit of talk going around town about him,"

Longarm said truthfully. "I hear tell that some ship captains won't even sail the Gulf anymore because they don't want to run into that pirate ship."

"I don't know anything about that," Prescott said. "I'm a cattleman. I don't have any use for the ocean. But I'm from New England, Long. I'm hardheaded enough not to believe in ghosts."

"Can't say as I believe in 'em, either. But something's causing ships to sink."

Prescott waved a hand. "Not my worry. My only concern is stopping those rustlers from robbing me blind."

Clearly, Prescott saw no connection between his problems and whatever mystery was going on out in the Gulf. Well, maybe he was right about that, Longarm told himself. The two things didn't have to be tied together at all. His lawman's instincts still said it was possible, though.

Judith came back into the parlor. "Consuela says dinner will be ready in half an hour."

She had changed clothes while she was gone. Instead of the denim trousers and jacket she had worn earlier, now she was garbed in a high-necked, long-sleeved blue dress with lace at the cuffs and throat. It went well with her blue eyes.

And it was tight enough so that Longarm could see the intriguing curves of her bosom and hips. She was slender, but not as boyish as he had thought at first.

He became aware that his clothes were stained with mud and still a little soggy from the salt marsh. He said, "I don't know that I'm fit to sit down to dinner with you folks—"

"Nonsense," Prescott said. "We can come up with some clothes for you to wear, if you'd like to change."

Judith took his arm. "I'll take Mr. Long up to one of the guest rooms, Father."

Prescott nodded. "Get him some clothes from Adrian's room."

Judith steered Longarm out of the parlor toward a flight of stairs. As they started up, Longarm glanced over his shoulder and saw Chuck Ballinger leaning in the entrance to the parlor, watching them with narrowed eyes. Ballinger obviously didn't like the attention that Judith was paying to the visitor.

Longarm found it more than a little odd himself. It hadn't been that long ago that everybody on the whole damned ranch had been ready to kill him. At least, it had seemed that way at the time. Now, all of a sudden, they couldn't do enough for him.

Maybe he was just being too suspicious. Maybe they had realized that they were wrong about him, and now they were trying to make up for what had almost happened. Longarm was willing to admit that possibility, but he wasn't convinced of it yet.

"Who's Adrian?" he asked as they climbed the stairs.

"My brother," Judith replied. "He's no longer with us, though."

"You mean . . ." Longarm didn't much cotton to the idea of wearing a dead hombre's clothes, although he had done it before.

"I mean he's back in Boston with our mother. Both of them hate Texas and only visit when my father insists on it."

"Oh." He paused, then went on, "I reckon that means you like it here?"

"Of course. I love to ride, and rope cattle, and shoot. I'd positively stifle in Boston if I had to live there."

Longarm figured he would, too, but he didn't say as much.

"Adrian keeps some clothes here for his occasional visits," Judith went on. "You and he are about the same height. His shirts are going to be tight on you, though. Adrian's chest and shoulders aren't nearly as, uh, muscular."

She looked over at him and smiled. Lord, he thought, now she was flirting with him! An hour or so earlier she had thrown lead at him, then cussed a blue streak as she

70

fought with him. Now butter wouldn't melt in that pretty mouth of hers.

There was just no figuring out women.

She took him to one of the bedrooms on the second floor and said, "Wait here, and I'll see what I can find. I'll send one of the maids in with the clothes."

"I'm much obliged." Longarm hoped it would be Consuela, but that was unlikely since she seemed to be in charge of dinner.

Judith gestured toward his feet. "Take those boots off, too, and I'll have them cleaned." She left, closing the door softly behind her.

Longarm peeled off his muddy shirt and dropped it in a corner where the mud wouldn't get on the rug. He tried balancing on one foot while he took the other boot off, but that was awkward and the boot was too stubborn to come off easily. He didn't want to sit down on the bed, though, because if he did, he would get mud on the comforter.

There was only one solution. He unbuckled his gunbelt with its now-empty holster and hung it over one of the bedposts. Then he unfastened the belt around his waist and unbuttoned his trousers. He lowered them around his ankles and sat down on the bed wearing the bottom half of his union suit. Now he could get the boots off.

He had just started working on that when the door opened and Judith stepped into the room again with a shirt and a pair of trousers draped over her arm. She hadn't sent one of the maids after all but had brought the clean clothes herself. She stopped short at the sight of Longarm's bare, muscular chest with its thick mat of dark brown hair. Her eyes widened.

"Oh, my goodness," she said.

Longarm suddenly had a bad feeling about this.

Chapter 10

Sure enough, Judith dropped the clothes on the floor at her feet and pushed the door closed behind her. She came across the room toward him, still eyeing his chest. Her gaze dropped down to the considerable bulge at his groin outlined by the union suit, and he thought he heard her catch her breath.

"Do you need some help, Mr. Long?" she asked, her voice husky. She seemed to catch herself with a little shake of her head. She went on in more normal tones, "With your boots, I mean?"

"I reckon I can manage," he said, acutely aware that he was mostly undressed.

"Nonsense. Let me give you a hand." She turned her back to him, bent over, reached down, and grabbed his right foot. She pulled his leg up between hers and braced it there as she began tugging on the boot.

From this angle, Longarm had a mighty nice view of her backside. He said, "Be careful you don't get mud on your dress."

"Oh, I'm not worried about my dress. If it gets muddy, I'll just take it off."

Longarm didn't doubt that for a second.

She pulled at his boot for a moment, then said, "You

know, it would help if I had something to lean back against."

"I, uh, can't get my other foot out of my trousers until the boot's off."

"I know that. Use your hands."

"I ain't sure that's such a good idea . . ."

She smiled at him over her shoulder. "Oh, come now, Mr. Long. I'm sure you've touched a woman's derriere before."

"Yes, ma'am, I reckon." Longarm leaned forward and put both hands on her rump, giving her something to push against as she tried to pull off his boot. He assumed as slim as she was, she must be corseted up pretty good under that dress, but he found to his surprise that her figure was natural. He didn't feel any whalebone under the dress, just woman.

His right boot came free. Judith stumbled forward a step before catching herself. "Now for the other one." She backed up to him again, and he put his hands on her rump again.

If Prescott happened to come in now, he'd be getting out his shotgun again, Longarm thought.

"You know, I ain't sure how proper this is."

"In my opinion, people spend entirely too much time worrying about what's proper and not nearly enough making sure that they enjoy life." The other boot came off. Judith dropped it and turned around. "Now for your trousers."

They were already down around Longarm's ankles, but he stood up and yanked them back to his waist. "I can manage now, ma'am," he said. "I'm much obliged to you for your help."

"But I can't leave yet," Judith said, all wide-eyed innocence. "I don't know if the clothes I brought you will fit."

"I'm sure they'll be fine."

"You act embarrassed, Mr. Long. You shouldn't be.

73

I've seen gentlemen in a state of undress before, you know."

"Is that right?"

"It certainly is. Probably not as many as that little Antonia minx from Miguel's, though. She was the one Brick was talking about, wasn't she?"

Longarm didn't want to have this conversation, but he didn't see any way of avoiding it. "That's right."

"I don't blame her. I wouldn't want to have anything to do with Brick Dunn, either. He's a crude, violent man. You, on the other hand . . ." She rested the fingertips of one hand on his chest. "I'll bet Antonia just ate you up, Mr. Long."

Longarm was only human. Good idea or not, he was about to put his arms around her and kiss her when she suddenly twirled away from him. She went to where she had dropped the clothes just inside the door and picked them up.

"Here," she said as she tossed the shirt and trousers to him. "You're right, they'll probably fit, at least as close as we'll be able to find around here. No one else on the ranch is as big as you, Mr. Long." She reached into a pocket of her dress and brought out his Colt. "Come downstairs when you're done. I'm sure dinner will be ready by then."

She went out after handing over the revolver, and the door clicked shut behind her.

Longarm heaved a sigh of mingled relief and frustration. He was aware that Judith had been deliberately teasing him, and normally he didn't like that sort of behavior in a woman. Now, though, he was just glad she'd had the sense to stop when she did.

The trousers fit fairly well. They were a little short, but not much. The shirt was tight in the shoulders and chest, as Judith had predicted. Longarm thought it would be all right as long as he didn't move around too quick.

He buckled on his gunbelt, unwilling to leave it behind. He didn't anticipate getting into any gunfights in the Prescott dining room, but a fella in his line of work couldn't be too careful.

He left the room and went downstairs in his sock feet. His socks were still wet, and he wished he had asked Judith for a dry pair. But he could live with the slight discomfort, he decided.

Judith was waiting for him at the entrance to the dining room. "You look fine, Mr. Long," she said. She offered him her arm, and he took it. When they entered the dining room, he saw that Chuck Ballinger was gone. He had probably returned to the bunkhouse to eat dinner with the rest of the hands.

Hiram Prescott sat at the head of the long table, which was covered with a fine linen tablecloth. Two places were set at his right. Longarm held the chair next to Prescott for Judith, then took the seat beside her.

"All right, Consuela," Prescott called.

Longarm tried not to be too obvious about studying Consuela when the woman came in. She was a few years older and a few pounds heavier than her cousin Antonia, but she was still a fine-looking woman. She wore a conservative gray dress as she carried in platters of food and placed them on the table.

The food was good: fried chicken, pot roast, potatoes, corn, black-eyed peas, greens, biscuits with plenty of honey and butter. Longarm and Prescott had wine with their meal, while Judith drank what appeared to be lemonade. Prescott ate in dogged silence for a while, but then he said, "I'd be glad to sell you some cattle, Mr. Long. Would you want them driven to the railroad in San Antonio?"

"That would be best," Longarm replied. "I ain't sure I could draw up a contract, though, considering all the trouble you're having at the moment."

Prescott put down his fork and glared. "What the devil do you mean by that?"

"Well, with this rustling problem, I don't know if I could count on you to supply all the stock I'd need, when

75

I needed it. Those packing houses in Chicago have to have a steady stream of cattle."

The rancher's palm smacked down on the table. "I told you, I'm a long way from being cleaned out! I can still supply more stock than you can handle, Long."

Longarm held up a hand and said, "I didn't mean any offense. Just speaking plain. From what I've seen, we could do a heap of business . . . once you get this rustling problem cleared up."

"It's just a matter of time," Prescott growled. "Sooner or later, all those wideloopers will be kicking at the end of a rope."

"Father!" Judith exclaimed. "That's hardly polite dinner conversation."

Prescott picked up his fork and jabbed the air in Longarm's direction. "He brought it up."

"That's right," Longarm agreed.

He didn't really care about Prescott's rustling problem, other than its possible connection with whatever was going on out on the Gulf. On the other hand, he felt a grudging liking for the old cattleman. Prescott was high-handed and cantankerous, but maybe he had a right to be, considering that he had built himself a cattle empire.

And he had to deal with a spitfire of a daughter like Judith, which made Longarm feel even more sympathetic toward him.

"If you want to take a better look at the ranch after we eat, I'd be glad to show you around," Prescott offered.

"I'll take you up on that." Longarm would try to steer Prescott toward the coast, so that he could familiarize himself more with the area where the so-called pirate ship had been seen.

Consuela had been in and out of the dining room several times during the meal. Now she leaned over the table and picked up an empty bowl to take it back to the kitchen. As she turned away, Prescott said, "I don't reckon you'll see any pirates' ghosts, though."

The bowl slipped from Consuela's fingers and crashed to the floor.

"Damn it, woman!" Prescott exploded. "What's wrong with you? Be careful!"

"*Sí, senor,*" Consuela said as she hurriedly bent to clean up the broken pieces of the bowl.

So she was touchy about any mention of Bloody Tom Mahone, Longarm thought as the servant disappeared back into the kitchen. If he did get a chance to ask her about the incident, he would have to be careful. He had a feeling she would spook easily and might refuse to talk to him.

That would have to wait, though. Right now he had to deal with Prescott. He would continue to stall the cattleman on any potential deal and at the same time try to find out as much as he could about the rustling and its potential tie-in with the case that had brought him here.

When the meal was over, Prescott suggested brandy and cigars before they rode out. Longarm agreed, and the rancher took him into an office paneled with dark wood. Longarm already knew the brandy was good. The cigars were, too, although to tell the truth he preferred his own three-for-a-nickel cheroots.

"I'm sorry about pulling that shotgun on you earlier," Prescott said as he puffed on his cigar. "I suppose I let myself get too hotheaded. You'd think by now I'd know to take most of what Judith says with a grain of salt."

"Well, I *did* take a shot at her, knock her down, and rassle with her," Longarm said with a smile. "I reckon most men would do the same thing you did if they heard about such things happening to their daughters."

"Yes, but Judith isn't like most daughters." Prescott sighed. "She's a bit headstrong and quick to anger. She's very stubborn about getting her own way, too."

Longarm didn't know what to say to that, so he just took another sip of brandy.

"I suppose it's been difficult on her, growing up out here without a mother," Prescott went on.

"She told me your wife lives back in Boston with your son?"

"That's right. Lillian never liked Texas, and neither did Adrian. They visit occasionally, but not very often. I still have some business holdings in Boston, and Adrian manages them for me. Does a fine job of it, too."

Longarm heard a touch of pride in Prescott's voice. The man's son hadn't chosen the life that Prescott would have picked for him, but the cattleman was still willing to give credit where credit was due.

"Lillian insisted that Judith live with her, too, and she did until she turned eighteen a couple of years ago. Then she came out here, and nothing her mother could say could persuade her otherwise." Prescott tossed off the brandy that remained in his glass. "I must say, I'm glad she's here, even though she can be quite a vexation at times."

"A man needs his youngsters around," Longarm agreed. He supposed that was true, even though he didn't have any children himself.

"Indeed he does." Prescott reached for a coat and a Stetson hung on a hook just inside the door. "Let's have that look around the spread—"

He stopped short, and Longarm heard the quickly indrawn breath of pain from him. He stepped to Prescott's side and saw that the rancher's ruddy face was even more flushed than usual. Prescott clenched his right hand into a fist and pressed it against his chest.

"Are you all right, sir?" Longarm asked.

"Damn . . . spasm," Prescott grated. "It'll pass, Mr. Long. Don't worry . . . about that." He grunted and bent forward, pushing hard against his chest with his fist.

Longarm started to turn away. "I'll get some help—"

Prescott's other hand caught his arm with surprising strength. "No! There's no need. I'll be all right."

"But your daughter ought to know."

"I'm asking you, Long . . . man to man . . . not to say anything to her. I don't want to scare her. It's just . . . a

78

palpitation . . . had them before . . . they come and go."

Prescott's face was shading toward gray now, but he was able to stand up straight again. "Get Judith to . . . show you around. She knows this ranch about as well . . . as I do. Tell her I have some work . . . I forgot about."

"You sure this is what you want?" Longarm asked with a frown.

"I'm sure."

Longarm felt uneasy about it, but he didn't see any choice except to honor the man's wishes. After all, he was a guest in Prescott's house and on Prescott's land.

He nodded and said, "All right. But you might want to see a sawbones about that."

"I'll do that one of these days." Prescott's color was a little better now, and the lines of pain on his weathered face had eased a bit. Longarm could tell that the spasm was tapering off. Prescott moved toward the desk and said, "I'll be fine. I just need to sit down for a while and have some more of that brandy."

Longarm nodded. "I'll be seeing you, then."

He left the office and went to look for Judith. He was certain she would be agreeable to showing him around the ranch. Of course, that would mean the two of them would be alone together again, and that was a mite worrisome.

He would feel a little better about it, Longarm decided, if he could be sure whether she would try to kiss him or shoot him.

He had a hunch that where Judith was concerned, a fella would just never know . . .

Chapter 11

Judith Prescott accepted without hesitation the story that Longarm told her about her father suddenly remembering some work he had to do in his office.

"I'll change clothes and be right with you," she said. She laughed and fluttered the skirts of her dress. "Can't very well go galloping around the ranch in this."

When she had gone upstairs, Longarm headed for the kitchen. He figured this would be his best chance to talk to Consuela.

The woman was in the kitchen, as he hoped she would be. She turned sharply when Longarm came into the room and regarded him suspiciously. "There is something I can do for you, señor?" she asked.

"Was looking for my boots," Longarm said, keeping his tone casual. "I think they were brought downstairs to be cleaned . . ."

Consuela relaxed a little. "*Sí, senor.* Your muddy clothes, too, but they are still wet."

"Don't need the clothes," Longarm said with a wave of his hand, "but I can't go riding without the boots. Miss Judith's going to show me around the ranch."

Consuela nodded. "I will get them for you. I think perhaps they are dry enough to wear."

"They'll be fine. But before you go, Consuela . . . Your

cousin Antonia in Corpus Christi suggested that I talk to you."

The slight frown of suspicion reappeared on the woman's face. "About what? I do not do the things Antonia does—"

"About Bloody Tom Mahone and his black-sailed ship," Longarm cut in.

Consuela stiffened, and she muttered something under her breath in Spanish that might have been either a curse or a prayer. Longarm decided it was a prayer when the woman crossed herself.

"I know nothing about such things," she said.

"Antonia told me you might have seen Mahone's ship," Longarm prodded.

"No. It is impossible." Consuela shook her head. "That hombre Mahone has been dead for many years, and his ship is no doubt on the bottom of the sea. I could not have seen it. I was mistaken."

"What if I tell you that I believe you really did see it?" Longarm asked.

Again Consuela crossed herself. "I . . . I do not believe in ghosts." From the tone of her voice, though, it was evident that she did.

"Maybe what you saw wasn't a ghost ship. Maybe it was real. If Mahone could rig a ship with black sails eighty years ago, there's no reason why somebody else couldn't do the same now."

Consuela came a step closer to him and said quietly, "You believe me? You do not think that I am mad?"

"I sure don't," Longarm assured her. "Why don't you tell me about what you saw? But make it quick, because Miss Judith will be looking for me to take that ride with her pretty soon."

Consuela nodded and launched into her story, a mixture of fast-paced English and Spanish. Longarm was able to follow what she was saying with no trouble, and the tale that unfolded was the same as the one Antonia had reported to him, only with a bit more detail, such as the

81

name of the cowboy who was with Consuela when she saw the mysterious ship.

"I tried to point it out to Rowdy," she said, "but the moon had gone back behind the clouds and he could see nothing. It was very dark, *es verdad,* but I know what I saw, señor. I do not lie."

"I reckon not."

"But if it was not a ghost ship, why was it there?"

"Chuck Ballinger thinks that maybe whoever has been stealing Diamond HP cattle is taking them away on a ship."

Consuela's eyes widened in understanding. "This could be true. I know little of such things. I just work here in the house, you know? Señor, why do you ask me these things? Are you a lawman?"

Longarm toyed with the idea of revealing his true identity and swearing her to secrecy, but he decided to continue keeping those cards close to his vest for the time being. "I'm just a cattle buyer," he said, "but it's to my advantage to help Señor Prescott clear up this rustling problem if I can. That way we can do business."

Consuela nodded, seeming to accept the explanation.

"Have you seen anything else strange out on the water?" Longarm went on.

She shook her head. "No, señor. Only the one time, in that cove. La *embrujada.*"

The haunted. Longarm thought that was a fitting name, considering what Consuela had seen there.

"Better get those boots," he said. "And thanks. If it's all right with you, don't say anything to anybody about this talk we had."

"No, señor, I will say nothing," she promised. She seemed glad that someone had believed her at last.

She fetched the boots from somewhere in the back of the house and gave them to Longarm. He sat down in the kitchen and pulled them on. As Consuela had said, they were still a little damp inside, but he could put up with that.

Longarm went out onto the porch to wait for Judith. He hadn't learned much from Consuela, he thought, but her story was added confirmation that something strange was going on along the coast.

He spotted Brick Dunn lounging in the shade of a tree over by the bunkhouse, smoking a quirly. Dunn glared and snapped the smoke away when he saw Longarm. He straightened, and for a second Longarm thought Dunn might stalk over to the big house and try once again to have that showdown. Instead, the redheaded cowboy turned and went back into the bunkhouse.

Longarm's eyes narrowed. He didn't think Dunn would try anything while he was riding around the ranch with the boss's daughter, but Longarm was going to keep an eye on their backtrail just in case.

Boot heels rang on the porch as Judith came out of the house. Longarm turned and saw that she had changed into clean denim trousers and a plaid shirt with a cowhide vest over it. Her brown Stetson was on her head, but she hadn't bothered to tuck her hair up into it this time.

And she wore her gunbelt again, too, with the .38 Colt riding easily in the holster.

He put his hat on as he followed Judith down the steps off the porch. "I'll have the boys saddle fresh horses for us," she said. "That livery stable mount of yours could use some rest after the ride out here, I imagine."

"More than likely you're right. Know a lot about horses, do you?"

She flashed a grin at him. "I know a lot about a lot of things, Mr. Long."

Longarm didn't doubt that for a second.

The Diamond HP was too vast a ranch for them to cover all of it in an afternoon's riding—or in several days, for that matter. Longarm figured they would stay within an area that was no more than an hour or so ride from the ranch headquarters. Judith pointed out several good-sized jags of cattle as they rode along trails she seemed to know well.

"These longhorns are ornery as they can be," she said. "But you probably know that already, since you work with cattle all the time."

"Yes, ma'am," Longarm agreed. "They're well suited to this brush country down here, though."

"Don't call me ma'am, or Miss Prescott, either. Judith will do fine." She gave a little shudder. "Not Judy, though."

Just like Sandra Nolan and her aversion to being called Sandy, Longarm thought. These South Texas gals were some of the best-looking females he had ever seen, but they sure didn't like nicknames.

They started out circling to the west, but by pointing and making innocuous comments like "Let's ride over there," Longarm gradually steered them back to the east, toward the Gulf. They were close enough so that he could hear waves lapping at the shore when he spotted a man on horseback some distance away.

Thinking that it might be Brick Dunn, he edged his hand toward the Winchester. The man was out of handgun range, but the repeating rifle could reach him if necessary.

Instead of trying to bushwhack them, however, the man wheeled his horse around and rode off in a hurry. Longarm pointed him out and said, "Is that one of your ranch hands?"

Judith shaded her eyes with a hand and studied the retreating rider. After a moment she shook her head.

"I don't think so. I don't recognize the horse or the man." A hard edge crept into her voice as she went on. "He's probably one of Shawcross's men."

Longarm hadn't heard of anybody by that name. He said, "Who's that?"

"The man I suspect of being behind the rustling. His name is Mort Shawcross. He has a small ranch on the edge of our spread. He doesn't run enough cattle to make a living, but he always has money, and he always has several hardcases hanging around with him. He's an outlaw, all right."

From the way she described the man, that sounded likely, Longarm thought. A lot of small ranchers made their living by scavenging off their larger neighbors. A lot didn't, of course, and were as honest as the day was long. But Longarm figured Judith might be right about Mort Shawcross.

The rider was out of sight now. Longarm and Judith continued on toward the coast, chatting amiably. When they came within sight of the water, Longarm said, "We're not far from the place we ran into each other this morning, are we?"

Judith laughed. "You mean the place where I took a shot at you?"

"Well . . ."

"It's about a mile back up the coast."

"I don't see how you keep track of where you are," Longarm commented. "All this coastline looks about the same to me."

"When you've been around here for a while, you can tell the difference. See that slough?" She pointed to a narrow band of water that extended inland and finally vanished in the thick grass. "That's the Devil's Finger. A mile south is Camelback Bay. Beyond that is Redfish Cove. There are half a dozen little coves and bays in every ten-mile stretch of coastline."

"Like I said, I don't see how you keep up with it."

Judith turned her horse's head. "Come on. I'll show you one of my favorite spots."

Longarm kept a close eye out as they followed the coastline. He saw no sign of Brick Dunn behind them, and no more mysterious riders who probably worked for Mort Shawcross put in an appearance. They passed a lot of cattle and even saw a couple of deer, small, graceful creatures that bounded off at the approach of humans.

They came to a peninsula that thrust out a couple of hundred yards into the water. It was dotted with clumps of live oaks, including several that stood near the very tip of the finger of land. The trees were quite gnarled and seemed to lean over backward. Longarm knew they had grown that way because of the near-constant wind from the Gulf.

Judith rode out to the end of the peninsula. "Isn't it beautiful?" she said to Longarm as she reined in and sat looking out over the blue-green waves that lapped at a narrow, sandy beach. The wind whipped her blond hair around her face.

"Mighty nice," Longarm agreed. "Does this place have a name?"

She turned her head and looked at him. "Pirate's Needle."

Longarm nodded, not really surprised. Everything seemed to come back to pirates sooner or later. "How did it come to be called that?"

"Look out there offshore," Judith said, pointing. "You can't really see them, but there are sandbars out there that come up almost to the surface of the water in places. It's like that all up and down the Laguna Madre. People say that in some places you could ride all the way across it on a horse, but I wouldn't want to try that. There are plenty of holes and channels that are deeper. In fact, there's a channel right off the tip of this peninsula. A ship could sail through there, but the captain would have to know where he was going. Like threading a needle."

Longarm nodded. According to Cappy Fitzgerald, Bloody Tom Mahone had known this coastline like the back of his hand. No doubt Mahone had known about Pirate's Needle and the channel that ran through here. Perhaps he had used it to escape pursuit during his buccaneering days.

And maybe now a different sort of buccaneer used it, too . . .

Judith swung down from her saddle and tied the reins to one of the gnarled oaks. She took off her Stetson and hung it on the saddlehorn. "I'll show you what I meant about this being one of my favorite places," she said as she slipped off the cowhide vest and then reached for the buttons of her shirt. "I love to go swimming here."

Longarm's jaw tightened. While he always regarded the prospect of a pretty gal taking off her clothes with interest, it was broad daylight. True, the thick growth of trees sort of screened off the tip of Pirate's Needle from the rest of the mainland, but he wasn't sure that nobody could see them out here.

"We just met a while ago, Miss Prescott," he reminded her. "I ain't sure it's fitting—"

"I told you, don't call me Miss Prescott," she interrupted as she spread her shirt open, revealing the small, graceful mounds of her breasts with their pale pink nipples. "I'm sure my father warned you about me, Mr. Long. I'm wild and headstrong and do whatever I damned well please. Well, it pleases me to go swimming and to have you watch me." She paused and then added, "It would please me even more if you took off your clothes and joined me."

Lord help him, he thought. He was actually considering it. The temptation grew even stronger as Judith took off her boots, peeled down her denim trousers, and stepped out of them. She turned to run out into the water, her slim, pale body beckoning him.

He was saved from having to make a decision by an interruption, but it wasn't a particularly welcome one. The sound of hoofbeats made him hip around in the saddle, and as he looked back along the peninsula, he saw Chuck Ballinger galloping toward them.

And judging by the look on his face, the foreman of the Diamond HP was mad enough to kill somebody . . . preferably somebody named Custis Long.

Chapter 12

Judith must not have heard the hoofbeats, because she continued cavorting in the shallow water just offshore. Shimmering droplets splashed around her and trickled enticingly down her sleek body. But as she turned back toward the shore and saw Longarm wheeling his horse around, she let out a gasp of surprise.

Ballinger brought his mount to a skidding halt and was out of the saddle almost before the animal stopped moving. He yanked his Winchester from its sheath.

"You damn bastard!" he shouted at Longarm, who watched Ballinger carefully but made no move toward his gun. "You accept the boss's hospitality, and this is how you pay him back!"

"You're jumping to conclusions for at least the second time today, old son," Longarm said. "Nothing happened."

"Nothing!" Ballinger repeated furiously. "Miss Prescott . . . well, she's undressed!"

Longarm ventured a glance from the corner of his eye. Judith was as naked as the day she was born, all right, but at least she'd had the good sense to hunker down in the water and cover up as much as she could.

"No sense in denying that," he said, "but I've still got all my clothes on, and besides that, I'm on a horse. If you'll stop and think about that, Ballinger, you'll see that you're wrong about what's going on here."

"Just because I got here in time to stop anything from happening," the ranch foreman shot back at him.

"Chuck, this is none of your business!" Judith called from the water. "You go on now, and leave us alone!"

"Like hell I will!" Ballinger raised the Winchester and levered a shell into the chamber. "Get off that horse, Long. Now!"

Longarm didn't move. "Just what do you have in mind?" he asked.

"I'm going to give you the thrashing you got coming to you. Either that, or I'll shoot you down like the dog you are."

Longarm sighed. He had thought that after the initial misunderstanding that morning, he and Ballinger had been on pretty good terms. Ballinger had even seemed like a reasonable gent.

Clearly, all that went out the window where Judith Prescott was concerned. Ballinger had a bad case of the calf's eyes for her. A fella like that could be levelheaded on every other subject, but not the one that was most important to him.

"I don't want to fight you, Ballinger," Longarm said.

"Won't be a fight. It'll be a massacre." Ballinger jerked the barrel of the rifle. "Unless you'd rather I just ventilated you and got it over with."

With a sigh, Longarm took his right foot out of the stirrup and swung down from the saddle. He tied the reins to an oak branch, then took off his gunbelt and hung it over the saddle.

"Chuck, I forbid this!" Judith shouted. "Leave Mr. Long alone! That's an order!"

"Sorry, Judith," Ballinger said. "If you want to have your pa fire me, you'll just have to go right ahead. For now, I've got to do this."

"You're a damned fool!"

Ballinger winced slightly at her harsh words, obviously stung by them. But he was determined to go through with this. He put the Winchester back in its saddle boot and took off his own gunbelt.

Longarm hung his Stetson on the saddlehorn and turned to face Ballinger. The foreman left his hat on as he balled his hands into fists and rushed toward the big lawman.

Longarm stepped aside easily as Ballinger swung a roundhouse punch at his head. He could have hammered a fist into Ballinger's side, but he didn't. He didn't want to hurt Ballinger, and he hoped that the man would tire himself out and give up the fight.

Ballinger grunted a curse as he caught his balance and threw another looping punch. Longarm avoided it as well, and Ballinger burst out with "Damn it, stop dancing around!"

"There's no need for this, Ballinger," Longarm said, still hoping that the man would see reason. "I'm not out to take Miss Prescott away from you."

"Chuck!" Judith cried from the edge of the water. "What did you tell him? I told you not to say anything to anybody about what we did!"

So there *was* something going on between the two of them, only from the looks of things Ballinger took it a lot more seriously than Judith did. Judith had been ready and willing to do some romping with Longarm, no doubt about that. And if Ballinger hadn't come along when he did—obviously having trailed them from the ranch head-quarters—that was exactly what would have happened, more than likely.

Ballinger charged again, swinging wildly, and Longarm realized that he was going to have to do more than dodge to end this battle. He dropped a shoulder so that Ballinger's fist went harmlessly above it. Then he crowded in on the foreman, hooking a left and a right to the belly. Ballinger gasped for breath as the punches doubled him over.

Longarm poised a fist for a quick knockout blow to the jaw, but Ballinger didn't give him a chance to throw it. Instead the man lowered his head even more and bulled forward, crashing into Longarm and knocking him backward. Longarm felt himself falling but could do nothing to stop it. He landed hard on the ground and lost some of his own breath.

The two men rolled in different directions, putting some distance between them. They came up on hands and knees at the same moment and pushed themselves onto their feet. Ballinger stood there for a few seconds, his chest heaving and his face dark with rage. Then he let out a yell and attacked again.

This time he was a little less wild about it and took his time as he swung several blows at Longarm's head and body. Longarm managed to block most of them, but a short jab got through and smacked into the side of his face below his left eye, jarring him. He hooked a right to Ballinger's sternum that rocked the foreman back, then followed it with a left that caught Ballinger on the chin. Ballinger wavered but didn't go down.

Longarm sensed he was about to have an advantage. While Ballinger was still unsteady on his feet, Longarm bored in and tagged him with a left-right combination. Somehow, Ballinger stayed on his feet.

Ballinger was growing desperate now and thrust a booted foot between Longarm's legs. Longarm stumbled over it, and that gave Ballinger the chance to tackle him. Both of Ballinger's arms wrapped around Longarm's waist as the man drove forward. Longarm fell with Ballinger on top of him.

A last-second twist of his hips allowed Longarm to avoid the knee that Ballinger tried to drive into his groin. Longarm heaved upward, arching his back off the ground, and threw Ballinger to the side. Longarm went after him, landing with a knee in his opponent's belly. He sledged a punch to Ballinger's jaw that bounced the foreman's head off the ground. Longarm raised his fist again, ready to smash it down into Ballinger's face.

A pistol cracked wickedly, making Longarm freeze.

He knew he wasn't shot. He turned his head to look back over his shoulder and saw Judith Prescott standing there, naked and dripping water, her .38 Colt clutched firmly in her hand. "Stop it!" she cried. "Stop it, or I'll shoot both of you idiots!"

Longarm didn't think it was very nice of her to call them idiots when she was the one who had provoked the fight, but he made a habit of not arguing with naked women, or with women who pointed a gun at him. Since Judith qualified on both counts, he lowered his arm and didn't throw the punch.

Instead he moved back and stood up, stepping away from Ballinger. The foreman sat up groggily and rubbed his jaw where Longarm had walloped him. Then his eyes widened as he looked at Judith.

"For God's sake, put some clothes on!" he yelled at her.

"Don't tell me what to do!" she shouted right back at him. "You're not my father or my husband, Chuck Ballinger!"

"Damn right! And I never will be your husband, you . . . you trollop!"

For a second Longarm thought she was going to shoot Ballinger for that. Her finger actually whitened on the trigger. But then she eased off. She said, "I wouldn't marry you if you were the only man in Texas!"

"A fella would have to be the last man in Texas to want you!"

This was getting them nowhere, Longarm thought, and he wondered briefly why he always wound up getting involved in all sorts of complications every time Billy Vail sent him out on a case. He said, "Miss Prescott, why don't you get dressed and go on back to the house with Ballinger? I reckon I've seen enough of the ranch."

"Don't let this meddlesome fool run you off, Mr. Long. I assure you, what I do is my own business." She added in a hiss, "And Chuck Ballinger has nothing to do with it!"

Ballinger clambered to his feet, picked up his hat, and slapped it violently against his leg. "She's right about that! I don't have anything to do with her!"

Longarm put on his hat and buckled his gunbelt around his hips. He looked down at himself. The too-small shirt that belonged to Adrian Prescott was ripped in numerous places. It had split during the fight. Longarm didn't want to go back to the Diamond HP headquarters to pick up his own clothes, though. He said to Ballinger, "If you'd have Consuela send my gear to the Nueces Hotel in Corpus Christi, I'd be much obliged. And tell Mr. Prescott that I'll be in touch later about doing some business with him."

"I reckon I can do that," Ballinger said grudgingly. He might be crazy-mad with jealousy, but he was still the foreman of the ranch and felt a duty to do his job. Longarm was counting on that, anyway.

"Mr. Long, you can't just leave me here with this . . . this barbarian!" Judith protested.

"Ma'am, I'm sure you'll be all right." Longarm swung up into the saddle. "Thanks for, uh, showing me around."

She had showed him a lot more than that and still was. The wind had pretty much dried her by now, but even though she was no longer wet, she was still nude and seemingly unembarrassed by it. Longarm tore his eyes away from the graceful curves of her slender body and the enticing tuft of pale hair at the juncture of her thighs. He turned the horse and heeled it into a trot, calling over his shoulder to Ballinger, "Whoever brings my clothes into town can bring my horse, too, and swap it for this one at the livery stable."

Ballinger lifted a hand in acknowledgment.

Longarm rode off Pirate's Needle. He heard Judith and Ballinger shouting at each other behind him. She was still capable of losing her temper and shooting the ranch foreman, but Longarm hoped it wouldn't come to that.

Instead, the angry voices suddenly fell silent. Curious, worried that the two of them might be trying to throttle each other, he reined in and looked back toward the tip of the peninsula.

The live oaks made it a little difficult to see what was going on, but after a moment Longarm made out the two figures and saw them merge into one. They weren't wrestling or fighting, though. Instead, Ballinger's arms went around Judith's nude form and drew her toward him. She came willingly and tipped her head back so that Ballinger could kiss her.

Longarm grinned to himself and shook his head as he clucked to his horse and put the animal into a trot again. He would be willing to bet that there would be more arguments between Judith and Ballinger in the future. They were both too stubborn for things to be otherwise.

But for now at least, they had kissed and made up, and Longarm was glad of that. He didn't want to stand in the way of true love, he thought dryly.

He turned the horse north and rode toward Corpus Christi.

Chapter 13

In two days he'd had three bruising fistfights, first with Mauler Larribee in the barroom of the Nueces Hotel on the previous afternoon, then the brawl in Miguel's Cantina that night, and now the scrape with Chuck Ballinger on the Diamond HP.

By the time he reached Corpus Christi at dusk, Longarm's bones and muscles ached enough so that he hoped the night would be peaceful for a change.

He went to his room in the hotel to change clothes, ignoring the looks that people gave his ripped shirt. When he had cleaned up, donned a fresh shirt, and slipped back into his brown tweed suit, he headed back down to the lobby. As he reached the bottom of the stairs, Cappy Fitzgerald came in the front door.

"There you are," the old salt said. "I was hopin' I'd find you. Sandy wants to see you."

"I was on my way to get some supper," Longarm said. "What does Miss Nolan want?"

"She didn't say, just asked me to scout you up." Cappy shrugged. "I reckon if you don't want to see her, that's your choice."

"I didn't say that. Where is she?"

"At her office, down by the docks."

"Lead on, MacDuff," Longarm misquoted.

Cappy led the way along Water Street, past some warehouses to a small, neat frame building with a sign over the door that read NOLAN SHIPPING. He and Longarm went inside to find Sandra Nolan sitting at a desk, scrawling figures on a piece of paper. She looked up and grinned.

"We can do it, Cappy," she said. "If we get that cargo to Vera Cruz, I won't lose the *Night Wind*. We might even make enough to finance another run over to New Orleans."

"I figured once you started cipherin', you'd find a way," Cappy told her, returning the grin.

Sandra nodded to Longarm. "Hello, Mr. Long. I suppose Cappy told you the good news."

Longarm looked over at the old-timer, whose grin took on a sheepish look. "Actually, he didn't tell me much of anything except that you wanted to see me."

"He didn't? Cappy, you're being modest. Although I suppose I should call you First Mate Fitzgerald?"

Longarm cocked an eyebrow quizzically.

Cappy shuffled his feet. "Yeah, I done told Sandy I'll take the job o' first mate. Not permanent-like, though. Just until she gets back on her feet."

"I reckon this means you found a captain?" Longarm said.

Sandra shook her head. "No. I'm going to take over as captain of the *Night Wind* myself."

Her tone didn't betray any degree of uncertainty, but Longarm thought he saw some uneasiness lurking in her eyes. "That's a big decision," he said. "Some men won't even go to sea on a ship with a woman on it, let alone take orders from one."

"I know. But Cappy has already put together a crew for me, and the men are willing to accept me as captain."

Cappy put in, "They're all old sea dogs like me. They may not like it much, havin' a gal as captain, but they're willin' to put up with it if it means they get to go back to sea."

Longarm understood now. "What you mean is that they can't get a berth on any other ship."

"Well . . ."

Longarm looked at Sandra. "Can you handle a ship like that?"

Her chin came up defiantly as she replied, "Of course I can. I grew up around ships."

"That don't mean you can command one."

She put her palms on the desk and came to her feet. "I said I can do it. I fully intend to do it, and the voyage will be a successful one. Just wait and see."

"And what was it you wanted from me?" Longarm asked.

"I thought you might like to have dinner with me, to help me celebrate saving the *Night Wind*."

Longarm felt a little abashed. He had thought that she was going to ask him again to join the crew. Under the circumstances, he decided not to point out that she hadn't really saved the ship yet. It would take a successful voyage to do that. He didn't want to throw cold water on her optimism and enthusiasm.

"Sorry. If the invitation's still open, I reckon it'd be my pleasure."

"I don't know." Sandra hesitated, then shrugged. "Why not? Let's go."

She came around the desk and offered Longarm her arm.

"You two young folks go on 'thout me," Cappy said as Longarm took Sandra's arm. "I got work to do. I plan to go over that vessel from stem to stern and make sure ever'thing's shipshape on her. Be most of the night doing that, I reckon."

"When do you plan to sail?" Longarm asked.

"Tomorrow," Sandra said. "There's no time to waste."

Evidently not, he thought. He still wasn't sure about the idea of Sandra captaining the ship with a crew full of old geezers, but maybe it would work. The veteran sailors would certainly know what they were about.

But Bloody Tom Mahone, or whoever he was, was still lurking around the Gulf. Sandra might be sailing into danger.

Longarm toyed with the idea of going with her, if she would still have him. But he also had the lead involving Mort Shawcross and the rustling on the Diamond HP to investigate. He couldn't be in two places at once, so he had to follow the trail that was more likely to pay off. Sandra would have to make that trip to Vera Cruz without him.

Cappy headed for the dock where the *Night Wind* was tied up, while Longarm and Sandra went to the restaurant where they had eaten the night before. As they waited for their food after they had placed their orders, Sandra said, "I suppose you still think it's a bad idea for me to take over as captain."

"That's your business," Longarm said. "I'm staying out of it. Just so you don't think I'm too prejudiced, though, I once knew a gal who was the captain of her own riverboat and did a damn fine job of it. And that was up in Alaska, on the Yukon River. That's mighty rough territory."

"You've been to Alaska? You get around, Mr. Long."

"Call me Custis. I reckon I've always been a mite fiddle-footed. I like to travel."

"Well, you don't have to worry about me," Sandra said. "With Cappy to help me, I'll do just fine. Actually, I tried to get him to accept the position of captain, but he flatly refused. As first mate, though, I expect he'll really be in command most of the time."

Curious, Longarm asked, "Why wouldn't he be captain? He must've been one on some ship, otherwise he wouldn't have that nickname."

Sandra nodded. "For many years, he was a fine captain. Sailed the seven seas and put in at every port from Liverpool to Macao. But then he lost a ship when it went down in a typhoon. There were only two survivors."

"And he blamed himself for the disaster?" Longarm guessed.

"Not so much for being caught in the storm. There was no way he could have avoided it. But he felt that he should have gone down with the ship. He was still on board when it broke up and sank, but one of his crew spotted him in the water and grabbed him. The man held on to Cappy and clung to a floating spar until another ship rescued them later that same night. Cappy was still unconscious and didn't even know he'd been saved."

Longarm shook his head. "Sounds to me like he doesn't have anything to feel guilty about."

"That's the way most people would look at it," Sandra agreed. "But not Cappy. After that he started drinking too much, became unreliable . . ." She shrugged. "He never captained a ship again, and still refuses to do so. But like I said, I intend to lean on him heavily."

Maybe it would work out, Longarm thought. He certainly hoped so.

A voice spoke from behind him. "Hello, Sandra."

Longarm looked around to see big, handsome Harrison Thorpe standing there.

"Hello, Harrison," Sandra said. "You remember Mr. Long?"

"Of course." Thorpe moved around the table and extended a hand to Longarm. "Good to see you again. I hope you're not sporting too many bruises from that encounter with Larribee yesterday."

"Reckon I'm fine," Longarm said as he shook hands. He didn't mention the other brawls he'd been in since arriving in Texas. Anybody who didn't know better would probably think he was a troublemaker, the way he found himself in a fracas every time he turned around.

"Would you like to join us, Harrison?" Sandra asked.

"No, thanks, I just finished eating. I saw you over here and wanted to say hello before I left, though." He frowned slightly. "What's this I hear about the *Night Wind* sailing tomorrow?"

"That's right. She'll be bound for Vera Cruz with a load of cotton and manufactured goods."

"But I thought Captain Morton quit."

"He did. I'm going to captain the ship on this voyage."

Thorpe's frown deepened. "Are you sure that's a good idea? I mean, I know your background in shipping, but the lack of practical experience—"

"I'll be fine." Sandra gave an exasperated sigh. "I'm getting a little tired of defending myself. Mr. Long doubted the wisdom of the idea, too."

"But it ain't none of my business," Longarm said, holding up his hands. "I know not to argue with a gal who's got her mind made up about something."

Thorpe chuckled. "Yes, it is rather futile, isn't it?" He reached down and clasped Sandra's right hand in both of his. "Good luck to you. If there's anything I can do to help, just let me know."

"Thank you," she murmured.

Thorpe let go of Sandra's hand—after holding on for a little longer than he had to, in Longarm's opinion—and then left the restaurant. Dinner arrived a moment later, and Longarm and Sandra were occupied with it for a while.

Full night had fallen by the time they were strolling down Water Street again. The breeze off the Gulf had died down a little, and it was a warm, pleasant night. Millions of stars shone overhead. Longarm almost forgot about being tired and sore and bruised.

He would have gladly walked Sandra home, but she insisted on going back to her office instead. "Just a few more details to go over," she said.

"I can wait," he offered. "A gal probably shouldn't be walking around down here this close to the docks after dark."

She laughed. "That's not necessary. I have a pistol in my bag, and I know how to use it."

He didn't doubt that.

"Besides," she went on, "most of the sailors and the

people who work down here know me. They won't bother me."

"Well, if you're sure . . . ," Longarm said as they came to a stop in front of the building where Sandra's office was located.

"I'm certain. Good evening, Mr. Long . . . Custis." She laid a hand on his arm. "It was a very pleasant evening, too."

"Yes, it was," Longarm agreed. Without thinking too much about what he was doing, he put his other hand on her shoulder and leaned down to kiss her.

She didn't pull away or act surprised, but at first she wasn't very responsive, either. Then after a moment her lips softened under his and with a soft moan deep in her throat she moved against him.

Her mouth was hot and sweet, and when his tongue thrust against her lips she opened them and welcomed it eagerly. Her body was molded so tightly against his that he had no trouble feeling the beating of her heart through their clothing. She slipped her arms around his neck and returned the kiss with mounting ardor.

But then suddenly she pulled away. Her hands flattened against his chest to hold him off. Longarm didn't force her. He let go of her and backed off a step.

"Didn't mean to offend you," he said quietly. "I reckon it's just the sea air and all them stars and the fact that you're a mighty pretty gal—"

She silenced him by resting her fingertips on his lips. "No, Custis. You don't have to apologize. I . . . I wanted that as much as you did. I wanted more. I . . . I've felt so alone . . . trying to keep everything going . . ."

He figured she was going to break down and cry. If she did, he would be glad to hold her and pat her on the back, and it wouldn't have to go any further than that if she didn't want it to.

But instead she took a deep breath and said in calm, carefully controlled tones, "I'm sorry. I'm being foolish. Please forgive me."

"Nothing to forgive," Longarm said honestly.

"I really do have to get back to work." She turned toward the door, then paused and looked back at him. "Will you come down to the docks tomorrow when the *Night Wind* sails and see her off?"

"Sure," Longarm said with a smile. "If I can."

"Thank you. Good night, Custis."

"Night."

Sandra went into the office. A moment later the window glowed yellow as she struck a match and lit a lamp. Longarm turned away and started up the street to the hotel.

Before he got there, though, he reversed his course and headed for Miguel's instead. He wanted to tell Antonia that he had talked to her cousin Consuela.

And if he happened to go with her back to that little cottage around the curve of the bay . . . well, so much the better.

Chapter 14

All the damage from the brawl the night before appeared to have been repaired, and the cantina was doing a brisk business again when Longarm walked in. Miguel was behind the bar. He gave Longarm a slightly nervous smile, obviously recognizing him and remembering that he'd been in the middle of the ruckus.

Antonia saw Longarm, too, and hurried over to greet him. Men's eyes followed her and regarded Longarm enviously as she gave him a big hug. Her dark nipples stood out prominently against the thin fabric of her low-cut blouse.

"It is so good to see you again, Custis," she said as she led him over to an empty table. "I will bring beer."

She scampered away to the bar. Longarm dug out a cheroot, flicked a lucifer to life on an iron-hard thumbnail, and set fire to the gasper. Antonia brought a mug and a bucket of beer back to the table and sat down next to him.

"I did not know if I would see you again," she said. "Did you ride out to Señor Prescott's ranch?"

He nodded. "I sure did, and I saw your cousin, too." He lowered his voice, even though he didn't think they would be heard over the buzz of talk and laughter in the cantina. "She told me about seeing that ship with the black sails."

Antonia leaned toward him, her dark eyes wide. "You believe her?"

"I sure do. Fact of the matter is, there's not a doubt in my mind about what she saw."

"But how can it be? Unless there really are such things as ghosts . . ."

"Or men who rig a ship with sails dyed black," Longarm said.

Antonia frowned. "But who would do such a thing, and why?"

"As for who, I ain't sure about that yet. But the why is easy. A ship with black sails can't be seen as easily at night when it slips into shore to pick up a load of rustled cattle."

Antonia's eyes widened even more.

"And if somebody does spot a ship like that," Longarm went on, "chances are they'd think they were seeing something that wasn't really there. Nobody wants people to think they're crazy, so most of 'em would never say anything about it."

"But the ships that Bloody Tom Mahone has sunk . . . ?"

"Vessels that came along in the wrong place, at the wrong time. The fellas behind this don't want any witnesses. That's why they would even risk sinking a government revenue cutter."

Longarm took a sip of the beer and frowned in thought. Talking it out this way with Antonia was helping him to see things more clearly, so he was glad he had come to the cantina. Another idea occurred to him.

"And it could be there's more to it than just the rustling," he went on. "Everybody's worried about the ships that have gone down and afraid of that so-called pirate's ghost. If the fellas behind this make it more difficult for folks to ship their goods, they can grab up more than their share of the business being done, just by being brave enough to keep sailing."

"But ships belonging to all the major lines have gone down. Everyone is afraid."

"Well, I don't have all the details worked out yet," Longarm admitted, "but I think I'm on the right track."

"What business is this of a cattle buyer, Custis?"

The blunt question made him frown. In his zeal to figure out what was going on, he had gotten a mite carried away. Antonia might not be educated, but she was damn smart anyway.

"Let's just say I got good reasons for wanting to get to the bottom of this," he told her. He added, "And I sure appreciate the help you've given me so far."

Antonia still looked curious, but she nodded in acceptance of his answer. "*Sí*, Custis. I will ask no more questions. And anything I can do to help, you have but to ask."

He sat with her for a while, drinking beer, chatting, and turning over the half-formed theory in his mind, until she took his hand and ran her fingertip around the palm. Then she threw back the screen of dark hair that fell in front of her face and let her tongue dart out and lick over her lips.

The whole thing was pretty doggoned blatant, Longarm thought, but hell, when it worked so well, why not? He was about to suggest that they go back to her cottage when several men swaggered in through the beaded curtain that hung over the cantina entrance.

Antonia glanced toward them and frowned. "We should leave, Custis," she said quickly. "Those are bad men. Sometimes they cause trouble."

Longarm studied the newcomers curiously. The leader was a tall, thick-bodied man with a rawboned face. When he loudly ordered beer for himself and his men, his voice was scratchy, as if his throat had been injured sometime in the past. He wore range clothes and a wide-brimmed Stetson, as did his hard-faced companions.

"Who is he?" Longarm asked.

"His name is Shawcross. He calls himself a rancher, but I believe he is an outlaw."

So that was Mort Shawcross, Longarm thought. It was a stroke of luck that the man had happened to come into Miguel's tonight. Maybe it wasn't really such a coincidence, though. Cowboys from the ranches around town often came to this waterfront cantina. Shawcross and his men probably dropped into Miguel's fairly frequently.

Longarm didn't make a move to get up, despite Antonia's urging. As soon as she had mentioned Shawcross's name, he had decided that it might be worthwhile to keep an eye on the man and his companions. Sure, he was tired and sore and would have liked nothing better than a little loving with Antonia followed by a good night's sleep, but this was too good an opportunity to pass up.

He nursed his beer while Antonia kept casting worried glances toward the men at the bar. "I can tell you are thinking something, Custis," she said. "What is it?"

So far she had proven trustworthy, so he said, "I've got a hunch that fella might have something to do with the rustling going on out at the Diamond HP. If that's true, he might be tied in with whoever's pretending to be Bloody Tom Mahone."

"*Dios mío*," she breathed. "It could be true. I have heard rumors that Shawcross steals cattle, but no one has ever been able to prove it."

Longarm took another swallow of beer. "Maybe the right fella ain't tried yet."

Antonia lowered her voice even more as she said, "Custis, they are dangerous men. I . . . I would not want to see anything bad happen to you." Under the table, she rested a hand on his leg, sliding it up his thigh to his groin.

She made it mighty tempting to forget all about rustlers and ghost ships and pirates, he thought, as she squeezed and caressed his stiffening shaft through the fabric of his trousers. But as always, the job came first, and it was with a regretful smile that Longarm shook his head.

"Maybe later," he said. "Right now, I got to keep an eye on those old boys."

Antonia's face darkened with anger. She didn't like being turned down, and she didn't like Longarm putting himself in danger. "Perhaps I should find a man more appreciative of my charms," she suggested with a toss of her head.

"I'll sure miss you if you go, but I reckon you should do whatever you think is best," he told her.

She relented, catching up his hand and pressing the back of it against her cheek. "I cannot stay angry with a man such as you. But you must promise me, Custis, that whatever you do, you will be careful."

"I always am," he said.

Otherwise, he added to himself, he wouldn't have lived near this long.

Mort Shawcross and his men guzzled beer at the bar for a while, then moved to a table and played cards with a couple of sailors. The game was a peaceful one, though from time to time one of the cowboys would exclaim profanely when he won or lost a particularly big pot.

At a gesture from Miguel, Antonia got up from the table where she sat with Longarm and moved to the dance floor. The elderly guitar player strummed the strings while Antonia enthralled the customers with her dancing. No one tried to molest her tonight. Longarm figured the brawl from the night before was still on the minds of some of the patrons.

Shawcross and his men clapped and hollered when Antonia was finished. Then they turned their attention back to their poker game.

She came over to the table where Longarm sat. Her face was flushed and she was breathless from the dance, which she had flung herself into with great abandon.

"Did you watch me?" she asked as she sank into a chair. "Or did you watch Shawcross and his men watching me?"

Longarm grinned. "Oh, I might've spared you a glance or two. I never saw anybody dance prettier."

She smiled in spite of her annoyance with him.

A short time later, Shawcross and his companions picked up the money they had won and went back to the bar for a final drink before they sauntered out of the cantina. Longarm gave them a moment, not wanting to make them suspicious by following them out immediately.

Antonia caught his hand. "Remember your promise, Custis. Be careful."

He nodded as she squeezed her hand.

"Any señorita who cares for you must learn not to worry, I think," she said with a sigh as he stood up.

Without appearing to watch Shawcross and his men, Longarm had taken note of which way they turned when they left the cantina. He ambled in that direction himself. Across the way, starlight sparked reflections off the water, tiny bursts of light made to wink by the motion of the waves. They reminded Longarm a little of gun flashes.

The night was quiet and peaceful, though, quiet enough for him to hear the thud of hoofbeats as several riders headed south out of town. That would be Shawcross's bunch. Longarm turned and hurried back to the livery stable.

The old hostler grumbled about being rousted out of bed in the office, but he led out a fresh horse for Longarm. Longarm slapped his center-fire McClellan rig on the mount and pressed a coin into the old-timer's hand. Then he rode out and turned south, as Shawcross and the others had done.

He didn't get in a hurry, not wanting to ride right up the backsides of his quarry, but he didn't dawdle. As the lights of Corpus Christi fell behind, he followed the coast road, his keen eyes searching intently for the men he was after. In ten minutes or so, he spotted them up ahead and pulled his horse back to an easy walk.

Following someone at night like this was tricky. If he could see them in the moonlight and starlight, then they could see him. But if they didn't suspect they were being

trailed, they had no reason to turn around and look . . .
other than the natural caution that most Westerners pos-
sessed.

And if Shawcross and his men really were rustlers,
they would be even more careful. Longarm hung back as
far as he dared. Four horses made more noise than one,
so he tracked them as much by sound as by sight.

Before they reached the boundary of the Prescott ranch,
the riders veered off the road to the left, toward the Laguna Madre. Longarm frowned at that. According to what
Judith had told him, Shawcross's ranch was inland from
the Diamond HP. Shawcross and the others weren't
headed home yet.

But where were they going? Four men couldn't rustle
very many cattle by themselves, but Longarm supposed
they could cut out a small jag.

He heard waves lapping at the shore up ahead, the
sound obscuring the noises made by the riders. He had to
risk getting closer. Spotting the four men moving along
the shoreline, he followed.

After several miles, Longarm concluded that they were
now on Diamond HP range. Obviously, the barbed wire
boundary didn't reach all the way to the coast, because
he hadn't seen any sign of it. Cattle probably wouldn't
stray through this marshy, slough-cut country, though.

The trail ran in and out. Several times he almost lost
it. Longarm cursed under his breath. In the dark like this,
it would be easy for a man who didn't know where he
was going to blunder into one of the little coves.

Suddenly, the smell of tobacco smoke drifted to his
nostrils. He reined the horse to a stop in the shadows of
a small clump of live oaks and sat motionless in the saddle. The fact that somebody was having a smoke somewhere close by told him that Shawcross had stopped.
Longarm didn't know why, but he had a feeling he was
going to find out.

He slipped down from the horse's back and tied the

reins to a tree trunk. His hand closed over the animal's muzzle to keep it from calling out to the other horses that were nearby. As he stood there in the shadows, he studied the landscape around him.

To the left, moonlight shone on the water. To the right was the coastal plain, covered with saw grass and dotted with thorn brush and clumps of trees. Directly ahead of him was more water where the shoreline took a jog inland to form a small bay.

After a moment, Longarm spotted the tiny, telltale glow of cigarette ends under one of the trees beside the bay, about a hundred yards away. Shawcross and his men were waiting there for something.

A rendezvous with somebody? That was possible, Longarm thought. Or they might be waiting to bushwhack somebody, although that was less likely in his opinion. Whatever the reason, he intended to stay here until he found out what it was.

He didn't have to wait long. Less than a quarter of an hour later, he heard a creaking and popping that he recognized as the sound of sails filled with wind. He stiffened, and what felt like an icy finger traced a path along his spine.

Longarm turned his head to stare out over the water. He saw the ship coming into shore, a rakish, three-masted vessel that cut smoothly through the waves, carried along by the wind that filled its midnight-black sails.

Chapter 15

Longarm's heart thudded heavily in his chest. For a moment, he could have almost believed that what he saw was a ghost ship, manned by a crew of pirates who had been dead for scores of years. He closed his eyes, and an image filled his mind of bony, skeletal hands clutching the ship's wheel, of naked skulls with colorful kerchiefs wrapped around them, jaws leering in permanent, obscene grins.

Of course, that was crazy, and as soon as he took a deep breath, he was able to shove those thoughts out of his head. He understood, though, why people who had caught sight of the ship thought there was something supernatural about it. He knew why Consuela had crossed herself at the mention of Bloody Tom Mahone.

But whoever was sailing that ship, they damn well had to be flesh and blood.

And unless he missed his guess, they were bound for a palaver with those four rustlers who waited on shore.

Longarm had no doubt now that Shawcross was behind the rustling that had plagued the Diamond HP. There was no other reason for him and his men to be out here waiting for the mystery ship. The vessel tacked closer to shore and then dropped anchor. Longarm heard the faint splash as a small boat was put in the water. Oars squeaked in oarlocks as it was rowed ashore.

He had to get closer, otherwise he wouldn't be able to hear what was going on. Hoping that the rented horse wouldn't decide to let out a whinny, he catfooted toward the bay, staying in the shadows of the trees where it was possible, crouching low in the tall grass where it wasn't.

A voice called out. Longarm couldn't make out the words, but he recognized the gravelly tone that belonged to Mort Shawcross. A deep voice answered him. The voice of Bloody Tom Mahone?

Longarm bellied down and crawled closer. He estimated that he was no more than twenty yards from the men at the edge of the water. He took off his hat, parted the grass a little, and raised his head just enough to peer toward the spot where the rendezvous was taking place.

With a scrape of hull against shoreline, the boat grounded. A man stood up and stepped out of it. Longarm's teeth grated together. There was enough moonlight for him to see that the man wore a long coat, and an old-fashioned three-cornered hat rested on a tangle of thick black hair. He was tall and seemed to be heavily muscled, though it was difficult to be sure of that due to the enveloping coat. A bushy black beard stuck out from his belligerent chin.

The man looked like a pirate, all right.

He also looked like Mauler Larribee.

That knowledge flashed through Longarm's brain. He couldn't see well enough to be sure that the commander of the black-sailed ship was Larribee, but it was certainly possible. Did that mean that Harrison Thorpe was in on the scheme, or had Larribee cooked it up on his own, betraying his employer? Longarm recalled that one of Thorpe's ships had gone down, too.

He was close enough to hear what was being said now.

"Why'd you call us here tonight?" Mort Shawcross demanded. "You know we ain't got no more cattle yet. Ain't

112

plannin' to hit Prescott's herd again until a couple o' nights from now."

"That's why you're here," the big, bearded man said in powerful, rumbling tones. It sounded sort of like Larribee's voice, Longarm decided, but not exactly. Of course, Larribee could be disguising his voice. "You need to wait about rustling any more cattle. We can't meet you as scheduled two nights from now."

"Damn it, why not?"

"You work for me, not the other way around, Shawcross," the bearded man said. "You'd do well to remember that."

Longarm sensed the tension in the air, saw the way the outlaws and the sailors who had brought the boat ashore were regarding each other with suspicion. Clearly, there was friction between the two groups, even though they had been working together to loot Hiram Prescott's stock.

"All right," Shawcross finally said, and the tension eased a bit. "We'll wait until you let us know you're ready 'fore we hit the old man's herd again."

"That would be wise." Mahone, or Larribee, or whoever he was, paused and then went on. "Just for your information, Shawcross, I'll be busy the next few days going after another ship."

Shawcross gave an evil chuckle. "So there's still somebody who ain't too scared of you to go out on the Gulf, is there?"

"Yes, but when the *Night Wind* goes to the bottom of the sea with all hands, people will finally know not to dare the wrath of Bloody Tom Mahone!"

Longarm's pulse hammered wildly in his head. Sandra Nolan and her ship were the latest targets of this self-styled pirate! A part of him wanted to leap up and open fire on the bastards, but he knew he couldn't do that. He was a lawman, after all, and had to do things legal-like if at all possible.

Not only that, but if he remained in concealment until this meeting of villains broke up, he could hurry back to

Corpus Christi and get there in plenty of time to keep Sandra from sailing on the *Night Wind*. She would probably argue with him, but once he told her who he really was, she wouldn't have any choice.

Then he could arrest Larribee and Thorpe, get the local law to help him raid Shawcross's ranch, and start sorting out who was responsible for what. He might not be able to bag Larribee right away if the black-sailed ship was already somewhere out at sea, but sooner or later the big man would wind up behind bars.

"You like playin' pirate, don't you?" Shawcross was saying. The rustler laughed.

Mahone—Longarm had started thinking of him that way—reached down to his side, and steel rasped against brass as he drew an old-fashioned cutlass. Shawcross stepped back, his hand dropping to the butt of the gun at his hip.

Mahone didn't threaten Shawcross with the cutlass, though. Instead he laughed and said, "How do you know I'm playing a role, Shawcross? Perhaps I really *am* Bloody Tom Mahone, come back to life to have my revenge and find my treasure!"

With a hiss, the cutlass cut through the air as Mahone swung it back and forth. He laughed again.

"I don't care if you're loco enough to think you're old Jean Lafitte or Blackbeard hisself," Shawcross said. "All I know is we're gonna make a heap o' money when we get rid o' that herd you've got stashed down the coast. That's all I'm in it for."

Mahone thrust the cutlass back in its scabbard. "Keep following my orders and you'll be a rich man, all right," he said. "I'll send word when I'm ready to pick up more cattle."

With that he stepped back into the boat and sat down as his men took up the oars. They pushed off and began sculling back out to the black-sailed ship.

Longarm ducked lower in the grass and then lay motionless. He was well off the trail, so he thought Shawcross and the other outlaws could gallop away without noticing him.

They didn't mount up right away, though. Instead they stood smoking and watching the ship as the ebony sails were raised once more. The vessel came about and moved back out into the Laguna Madre. Within minutes, it was gone from sight.

Then and only then did Shawcross and the other rustlers swing up into their saddles. They were about to turn and ride away when a fresh set of hoofbeats sounded in the night.

The outlaws stopped and jerked their guns from leather as the rider approached. A man called, "Mort! Hey, Mort!"

"It's Tobe!" Shawcross exclaimed. "I had him come along behind us to watch our backtrail."

Longarm's jaw tightened as he lay there and listened. He was pretty sure the watcher Shawcross had set out hadn't seen him, but something had disturbed the man. A moment later he knew what it was.

"I found a horse back up the trail, tied in some trees," Tobe said as he rode up to the other rustlers.

Shawcross cursed. "You recognize it?"

"Nope. And it's got one of those Army saddles on it, not a range outfit."

"Some son of a bitch is spyin' on us!" Shawcross said. "Spread out, boys, and find him!"

Longarm bit back a curse of his own. He pushed himself up a little and reached across his body to draw the Colt from the holster on his left hip. There was still a chance that the rustlers might miss him as they searched in the dark, but he couldn't count on that.

The seconds dragged by slowly as he listened to the sounds that the men made as they looked for him. Their horses' hooves thudded against the soft earth, and the outlaws called quietly to each other. One of them rode within five feet of Longarm but didn't see him. Even after that close call had passed, he barely dared to breathe.

115

The voices receded, and he started to think that he had dodged this bullet. It was difficult to keep track of where all of them were, but he didn't think there were any close by.

"Mort, there's nobody out here," one of the outlaws said.

"Keep lookin'!" Shawcross insisted with a vicious edge in his voice. "That horse didn't tie itself up. Whoever rode it out here still has to be here!"

Suddenly, hoofbeats sounded behind Longarm. One of the outlaws had worked past him and now was coming back at a fast trot. Pure bad luck sent him across the open ground straight at Longarm with little or no warning.

Longarm had no choice but to throw himself desperately aside unless he wanted to be trampled. As Longarm rolled through the grass, the rustler yelled, "Mort! He's over here!" Colt flame bloomed in the darkness as the man stabbed a shot at him.

Too late to worry about hiding now, Longarm thought. He brought up his Colt and fired, the revolver bucking against his palm as flame geysered from the muzzle. The slug caught the rustler in the body and flipped him backward out of the saddle. He thudded to the ground, dying without a word.

Longarm sprang to his feet and lunged toward the dead man's horse. If he could get in the saddle, he still might be able to get away from Shawcross and the others. It was a slim chance, but the only one he had.

And it wasn't just his own life hanging in the balance. If he didn't make it back to Corpus Christi, Sandra Nolan would go sailing right into the deadly trap laid for her by Bloody Tom Mahone.

More gunshots ripped through the night as fangs of lead searched for him. He grabbed the horse's reins and tried to calm the animal, which was spooked by all the commotion. The horse danced around so that Longarm couldn't get a foot in the stirrup. He darted a glance over

116

his shoulder and saw the riders galloping toward him. Another bullet whined past his ear.

Finally, Longarm's foot found the stirrup and he hauled himself up into the saddle. He banged his heels against the horse's flanks and sent it lunging into a run. Twisting in the saddle, he triggered a couple of shots at his pursuers. Under the circumstances, he didn't expect to hit anything with the bullets, but he hoped the threat would slow them down a little.

Water splashed high around the hooves of the horse as it ran blindly into a shallow marsh. Longarm kept the animal moving, hoping that it wouldn't bog down in the mud. Reaching more solid ground, the horse churned on. Longarm leaned forward to make himself a smaller target. Shawcross and the others were still firing behind him.

Longarm sent the horse darting through a clump of trees, hoping that a low-hanging branch wouldn't sweep him from the saddle. After he was through, he heard a thump and a pained, startled cry behind him, and a glance back showed him that one of the rustlers' horses was now riderless. A grin tugged at Longarm's mouth under the sweeping mustaches. Somebody had had a run-in with a live oak branch and would be mighty sore come morning.

But that still left Shawcross and two more men, and they were as determined as ever to ventilate him.

He caught a glimpse of a slough in front of him and had to swing the horse hard to the left. A yell came from the outlaws behind him as they veered in that direction and cut the gap. Longarm kept his mount heading inland. He had to get away from the ragged edge of the coastline. It was just slowing him down.

He hoped, too, that the continuing gunfire might draw the attention of someone on the Prescott ranch. True, they were miles from the ranch headquarters, but some of the Diamond HP punchers might be out riding the range for some reason. It was unlikely but not impossible.

The horse began to labor underneath him. The animal had been galloping at top speed for several minutes now, and it was running out of sand. The only consolation was that the rustlers' horses had to be getting tired, too.

Longarm burst out of the grassy pastureland onto a road. This was the main trail that led to the ranch head-quarters, he thought. He hauled the horse's head around and turned left. The closer he got to the big ranch house, the greater the chance of finding some help.

Then, the sharper crack of a rifle sounded behind him. One of the rustlers had stopped and drawn a bead with a Winchester. With a heavy thump, the bullet smacked into the horse Longarm was riding. The horse faltered, and then its front legs went out from under it. It crashed to the ground, throwing Longarm.

He'd barely had time to kick his feet free of the stir-rups. The horse's fall sent him flying through the air. He slammed down with a bone-jarring, teeth-rattling impact that knocked all the air out of his lungs and left him half-senseless.

The part of his brain that was still working shouted urgently for him to get up and make a stand. He realized that somehow he had managed to hang on to the Colt. He rolled over, pushed himself to hands and knees, and started to lift the revolver.

It was too late. Shawcross and the other outlaws were already on him, surrounding him in the road. One of them kicked him in the jaw and sent him sprawling. Another booted foot came down hard on the wrist of his gun hand, pinning it to the ground. Longarm felt consciousness slip-ping away from him, but he was still coherent enough to be aware of the bulky shape looming over him, blotting out the stars.

"Throw him across a saddle and let's get out of here," Mort Shawcross's scratchy voice ordered.

Longarm felt hands grip him roughly and lift him, and that was the last thing he knew.

Chapter 16

One of the sickest feelings in the world was to wake up from being knocked out, tied belly-down over the back of a horse. Longarm knew that from experience, and it wasn't any better now than it had been any of the other times it had happened to him.

One thing you could say for it, though: It was better than being dead.

He was a little surprised to regain consciousness. As the horse rocked along, Longarm fought down the nausea that rolled through him and tried to make his brain work. He remembered Mort Shawcross ordering the other rustlers to pick him up and put him on a horse.

Why hadn't Shawcross just put a bullet through his brain? They had certainly been trying hard enough to kill him only moments before his horse fell and threw him.

The only answer Longarm could come up with was that Shawcross had decided to question him. The rustler boss must have decided that it would be a good thing to know who Longarm was and why he had been spying on them. They could always kill him later.

But not if he had anything to say about it, and he still might.

Longarm didn't let on that he was awake, even though he wanted to let out a groan of misery. He choked down the sickness, tried to ignore the agonized pounding in his head. He hoped fervently that they didn't have much farther to go.

In that respect, at least, he was lucky. Only ten or fifteen minutes after he regained consciousness, the group of riders came to a halt. Shawcross ordered harshly, "Get him off that cayuse and take him in the house."

One of the rustlers cut the ropes that passed under the horse's belly and bound Longarm's wrists to his ankles. Rough hands grabbed him and hauled him down. He made himself stay limp.

"Hey, Mort, the bastard ain't woke up yet. You reckon he's dead?"

"Can't you tell if he's still breathin'?" Shawcross demanded irritably.

"Well, I think so."

"Take him inside and dump him on the floor. Darnell, get a bucket of water. We'll wake the son of a bitch up."

Longarm could have saved them the trouble, but he wasn't in any mood to. He continued feigning senselessness as the rustlers carried him inside and dropped him heavily on a hard-packed dirt floor.

A minute later, a bucketful of water hit him in the face. It made him sit up, spluttering and gasping, but the cold shock of it also helped clear some of the cobwebs out of his brain. Longarm had been counting on that.

A boot hit him in the chest and drove him back down. He looked up, blinking and shaking his head to get some of the water out of his eyes. He saw Shawcross standing over him, resting a foot on his chest. Shawcross eared back the hammer of the revolver in his hand as he pointed it at Longarm's face.

"Who the hell are you?"

"Custis Long." Longarm's voice sounded rusty to his ears.

"That don't tell me diddly-shit. Why was you out there spyin' on us?"

"I wasn't spying on you. Didn't even know you boys were around until you jumped me."

Shawcross leaned closer and sneered. "You go to lyin' and I'll put a bullet right up your nose, you son of a bitch. You killed one o' my men out there, you know that? Cole was a good man, and you shot him."

"He was trying to shoot me," Longarm grated out as Shawcross increased the weight on his chest.

The other three men crowded around. One of them held himself gingerly, and Longarm suspected he was the one who had run into the tree limb, maybe busted a rib or two. Longarm hoped so. He hoped it hurt like blazes, too.

One of the men spoke up. "I say we go ahead and kill him, Mort. Ain't no reason to keep him alive."

"No reason 'cept I say so," Shawcross snapped. "I want to find out how much he knows." The rustler boss leaned over Longarm again. "How about it, mister? You gonna talk, or do I see to it that you die a slow, mighty painful death?"

Longarm forced a laugh past his clenched teeth. "I been tortured by Apaches. I ain't afraid of anything you can do, old son."

"We'll just see about that." Shawcross straightened. "Search him while I think about what I'm gonna do to him first."

The other men went through Longarm's pockets. He had stashed his badge and bona fides in the hotel room back in Corpus Christi. The rustlers wouldn't find anything to identify him as a lawman.

His brain worked furiously, trying to come up with a story Shawcross might accept. When the men straightened from searching him, one of them gave him a light kick in the side and said, "Nothin' on him except a little cash, Mort."

Shawcross swung around with a fiendish grin on his face. "Heat up the stove and fetch one of the runnin' irons, boys. We'll practice alterin' brands on this ornery bastard's hide."

"Hold on," Longarm said, allowing a note of fear and desperation to creep into his voice. It wasn't all an act, either. He didn't doubt for a second that Shawcross was capable of taking a red-hot running iron to him. "There's no need for this. Hell, we're all in the same line of work."

"What do you mean by that?" Shawcross demanded with a frown.

"You wouldn't have running irons if you weren't doing some widelooping. That's why I'm here, too."

Shawcross stared at him. "You don't look like no rustler to me, dressed up in that fancy town suit."

"I've been pretending to be a cattle buyer. I was out at Prescott's ranch today, getting the lay of the land and checking out his stock. Rode back out there tonight to see if I could find a good way to get some rustled beeves away from there."

"That's a crazy story, Mort," one of the men said. "How many cattle could one man steal?"

"I ain't in this on my own," Longarm said. "I've got a gang just waiting for me to give them the word." He paused, then added, "They're liable to come looking for me when I don't show up at the hideout, and they're a gun-quick bunch."

Shawcross sneered again. "You're wastin' your breath if you're tryin' to scare me."

"Just telling you the way it is," Longarm said. "You told me not to lie to you."

"How do we know the whole thing ain't a lie?"

"I just admitted I intend to steal some cattle from the Diamond HP. You can take me to the sheriff and turn me in if you want. I don't think a fella would deliberately lie himself into a jail cell, do you?"

For the first time, Shawcross looked a little doubtful. What Longarm said made sense, if it wasn't examined too closely.

"Maybe you're tellin' the truth," Shawcross said as he rubbed a hand over his beard-stubbled jaw.

"He still killed Cole!" one of the rustlers protested. "And he was still spyin' on us!"

"I know better than to ride up on a bunch of fellas after dark," Longarm said. "That's a good way to get shot." He shrugged. "And hell, I admit I was trying to overhear what you were saying. I was curious. I never saw a ship like that before."

"What do you know about that ship?" Shawcross asked sharply.

"Not a damned thing. I never been around the ocean before."

"And you didn't hear what we were talkin' about?"

Longarm shook his head. "Never got that close," he lied.

"Aw, he's just tryin' to save his own skin, Mort!"

"Probably," Shawcross agreed. "But if he's tellin' the truth, there's another gang fixin' to try to move in on our deal. We can't have that. We'll hang on to this fella, and if that other bunch shows up, we can use him as a bargainin' chip."

The other men frowned, but they nodded in reluctant agreement. Longarm tried not to show the relief he felt. The longer they kept him alive, the better chance he had of getting away.

He didn't know how much time had passed, but he might still be able to make it back to Corpus Christi in time to keep Sandra Nolan from sailing on the *Night Wind*.

Only if he could escape from these outlaws, though . . .

Shawcross ordered him tied up. The rustlers did so, taking great enjoyment in jerking his arms behind his back and lashing his wrists together tightly. They left him propped in a corner of the room. He had a chance now to make a better study of his surroundings.

He was in a crude adobe cabin that he assumed was Shawcross's ranch house. It was little better than a Mexican jacal. A rough-hewn table sat in the center of the room, with empty crates lying on their sides to serve as chairs. There were bunks on the two side walls, a fireplace at the rear where the men would do their cooking, and one door in the front, flanked by a window on each side. A single shelf held a few meager supplies. The glow from a lamp on the table lit the room.

"It's late," Shawcross announced. "Reckon we'll all turn in, 'cept for one man guardin' the door. Tobe, you take the first shift."

Tobe didn't look too happy about that assignment, but he nodded. "Sure, Mort." He kicked one of the empty crates over beside the door and sat down on it, leaning his back against the wall.

Shawcross turned down the wick on the lamp until only a tiny flame was left. He and the other two men crawled into their bunks.

Longarm was in the corner next to the fireplace. One man's bunk was on that side of the room. Shawcross and the other man were on the far side of the room. Within minutes, all three of them were snoring heavily. From his post by the door, Tobe glared at Longarm.

Slowly and carefully, so that the motions wouldn't be noticed, Longarm felt around behind him, searching for something that he might use to cut the ropes around his wrists. There didn't seem to be anything within reach that might help him. But he couldn't give up. His life, and the lives of Sandra and Cappy and everyone else on the *Night Wind,* depended on him.

Tobe's eyelids drooped as he tried to fight off sleep. When the rustler's eyes closed for a few seconds, Longarm risked squirming closer to the fireplace. He froze as Tobe's eyes flickered open. A casual glance wouldn't reveal that he had moved.

Longarm was sleepy, too. It had been a long, difficult, dangerous day. But he knew he couldn't afford to doze off, and that urgency kept him awake. Every time Tobe started to nod, Longarm edged closer to the fireplace.

It was made of stone mortared together with adobe, and he had already spotted a piece of rock that looked like it might be loose. If he could get his hands on it and pry it free, the edge might be sharp enough to saw through the ropes. He knew that was his only chance.

More than an hour had passed. Longarm didn't know where they were, had no idea how long it had taken to reach here after the rustlers captured him on the Diamond HP. The time could be long after midnight. Every minute that slipped away was precious.

Tobe stood up, stretched, and went over to the one of the other men. "Wake up, Darnell," he said quietly as he shook the man's shoulder. "It's your turn to stand guard."

Darnell groused and grumbled but sat up and rubbed a hand over his thatch of pale hair. "If I got to get up, I'm gonna make some coffee," he declared.

"Go right ahead, just be quiet about it. You wake up Mort and you'll wish you hadn't."

Tobe crawled into his soogans and fell asleep immediately. Darnell stumbled across the cabin. He got a tin of Arbuckle's and a battered coffeepot from the shelf, dumped coffee and water from a jug into the pot, and brought it over to the fireplace. He leered at Longarm.

"Could get a mite hot, right here by the fireplace," he said.

Longarm ignored him. He finally had that piece of rock in his hands. He had gotten it while Tobe and Darnell were talking. When he tested the edge with his thumb, he found that it was sharp enough to scrape his skin. Whether it would cut through rope or not . . .

Well, there was only one way to find out.

Darnell kindled a small fire in the fireplace and put the coffee on to boil. Longarm felt the heat from the flames beating against his right side, which was only about two feet away. It was uncomfortable, but he thought he could stand it.

Darnell went back over to the door and sat down on the crate Tobe had vacated. Almost immediately, his eyelids lowered. These men might be good at rustling cattle, but they weren't much when it came to vigilance. Not that Longarm was complaining.

He went to work on the ropes, twisting and straining to get the sharp edge of the rock against them. Carefully, he began to scrape it back and forth.

He knew this was going to be a long, drawn-out job. Patience was the key.

After a few minutes, Darnell shook his head, opened his eyes, and got up to check the coffee. Longarm's eyes were mere slits, and he didn't move while the outlaw was near him. Darnell used a piece of thick leather to protect his hand as he lifted the pot and poured coffee into a tin cup. He replaced the pot at the edge of the fire and went back to the crate.

Longarm worried that the coffee would keep Darnell awake, but that proved not to be the case. As soon as the rustler finished the cup, he got drowsy again. He stayed awake for maybe five minutes before dozing off.

Longarm went back to work.

He couldn't help but scrape his wrists, too, as he sawed at the ropes. He felt blood trickling down over his fingers. He hoped he wouldn't cut an artery. That would be a damned stupid way to die, he thought, bleeding to death on the floor of an owlhoot cabin.

After so long a time, one of the strands of rope parted.

That gave Longarm hope, and he kept up the effort with renewed energy, stopping only when Darnell woke up enough to stretch and scratch a little before slumping against the wall again. The coffee was boiling away in the pot, but Darnell didn't seem to care.

Another strand of rope gave. Longarm bunched the muscles of his arms and shoulders and heaved, and his heart leaped as yet another strand parted. He twisted his blood-slick hands, and they came free.

But that wouldn't do him any good unless he could figure out a way to get past the rustlers. He didn't think he could slip out the door without waking Darnell, and the man had a rifle across his lap. Longarm figured that if he made a move, Darnell wouldn't hesitate to shoot him down, regardless of what Shawcross had said about keeping him alive.

What he needed was some way to get Darnell away from the door.

Longarm's legs were stretched out in front of him. His right foot wasn't far from one of the crates that the rustlers used as chairs. The crates were empty . . .

Yet this one wasn't.

Longarm's eyes narrowed. A tin can lay on its side inside the crate. The colorful label said that it contained tomatoes. Canned tomatoes were a favorite food of cowboys everywhere, even rustlers. Every ranch house, every chuck wagon, had a supply of airtights.

Longarm reached out with his foot, edging it closer to the can. The can might be empty, but if it wasn't, he could make use of it.

His toe touched the can. He rolled it toward him, and he could tell by the feel that it wasn't empty. The rustlers had simply overlooked it when they threw the crate down on the floor to use it as a chair.

As carefully as he had cut the ropes on his wrists, Longarm worked the can toward him. He had to keep his arms behind his back in case Darnell opened his eyes, and that was incredibly frustrating. All he had to do was lean forward and reach out, and he could have grasped the can. But if Darnell glanced at him while he was doing that, the jig would be up.

Longarm got the can under his leg. He drew his knee up and used his heel to push the can closer to him. Finally, it was close enough for him to risk snaking his fingers out to grasp it.

Darnell sat up, yawned, and took out the makings to build a smoke.

Longarm held the can close against his hip where Darnell couldn't see it. He pretended to be asleep. Darnell rolled the quirly, lit it, and smoked it while he stood up and stretched. Finally, he sat down again, dropped the cig-

127

arette butt on the floor, and ground it out with his boot heel. He crossed his arms over his chest and glowered at Longarm.

Slowly, his eyes closed again.

Longarm waited a minute just to be sure, then a flip of his fingers sent the can rolling into the fireplace. It made a little noise on the hearth, but not enough to disturb Darnell's slumber. Longarm twisted his neck to look into the fireplace. The label on the can had already caught fire and was burning.

The tin cans were called airtights for a good reason. When they were sealed up, no air could get in or out. But there was air in them to start with, and Longarm knew that when air got hot, it swelled up. That was how hot-air balloons worked. He licked his lips nervously as he watched the can. When it began to expand, he drew his legs up underneath him and got ready to move. His muscles were stiff, but they would have to work when he called on them.

Darnell snorted in his sleep. The noise was enough to disturb Mort Shawcross, who sat up and muttered, "What the hell—"

At that moment, the can of tomatoes in the fireplace blew up.

Chapter 17

Longarm exploded into action at the same instant, coming up off the floor as Darnell shouted and lunged across the room toward him. The loud report of the can blowing up made all the rustlers yell in confusion. It sounded enough like a gunshot that they must have thought they were under attack. At the same time, the juice from the can doused the flames, causing smoke to roll from the fireplace.

Darnell tried to lift the rifle, but Longarm got his hands on the barrel and shoved it back so that the butt smashed into the rustler's groin. Howling in agony, Darnell doubled over and let go of the Winchester.

Longarm's shoulder hit the door and knocked it open as guns blasted behind him. Bullets smacked into the adobe wall of the cabin, and some of the slugs chewed splinters from the door itself. Longarm went out in a rolling dive to one side. He came up in a crouch, reversed the rifle, and triggered four shots as fast as he could work the lever. He didn't expect to hit anything, but he hoped the lead flying around would make Shawcross and his men hunt for cover.

The pale light of dawn was beginning to spread over the eastern sky, Longarm saw as he came to his feet and dashed toward a pole corral built at the side of the cabin.

Several horses were milling around there, spooked by all the shooting.

Longarm flung aside the loop of leather that kept the corral gate closed and plunged into the enclosure. He didn't have time to saddle one of the horses, but he could manage just fine bareback.

The horses began to stampede out through the open gate. He reached up, grabbed the long mane of a sturdy sorrel, and vaulted onto the animal's back. A bullet whined past his head. The horse reared in fright, and Longarm hung on for dear life. When the sorrel's front hooves came down, it bolted.

Longarm lay flat along the horse's neck like a Comanche. Shawcross and the other rustlers howled curses and blazed away at him, but none of the hastily fired bullets found their mark. Guiding the horse with his knees, Longarm galloped out of the corral and away from the cabin.

The corral stood empty behind him, all the other horses having scattered.

He smiled grimly. It would take a while before the rustlers could round up those horses on foot and come after him. By then, he would have a big lead.

There was one problem: He didn't know where the hell he was or how to get back to Corpus Christi.

Longarm stayed low on the sorrel's neck and kept it running at a fast pace until at least a couple of miles had fallen behind them. Then he straightened and let the animal drop back to a trot.

The sun wasn't up yet, but there was enough light in the sky for him to be able to see his surroundings. Much of the landscape was covered with thick reaches of chaparral. This was the South Texas *brasada,* the brush country that stretched from the coastal plain to the Rio Grande Valley. Not good for much of anything except wild horses and the rangy longhorns that grazed on vast ranches like the Diamond HP.

Judith had said that Shawcross's ranch bordered on the Prescott range. Longarm realized that if he headed east, eventually he would reach the big ranch. From there he knew how to get back to Corpus. His spirits rose a little. After the hellacious night he'd just spent, his brain hadn't been working at full speed. He knew now that he could make it to the seaport town.

But it could take hours of riding to get there, and he wasn't sure when Sandra planned to sail. She had asked him to see the *Night Wind* off, and he had promised to do so. Would she wait for him if he didn't show up in time?

He didn't think so. Sandra was desperate to make that voyage to Vera Cruz and save the ship that was her legacy from her father. When the time came to sail, she would sail.

He kept an eye out behind him for any signs of pursuit but didn't see any. The sorrel was well rested and able to keep up a steady, ground-eating lope. The sun peeked over the horizon and then began its daily climb into the sky. The miles fell behind.

Longarm thought that he must be on Prescott range by now. He hoped to run into one of the cowboys who rode for Hiram Prescott, but so far he hadn't seen any signs of life except for cows and birds and a rabbit or two. The wind freshened, and he tasted salt on his lips. He was getting closer to the Gulf.

He spotted a broad trail through the chaparral ahead of him, and when he came to it he realized it was the road. Without hesitation he turned north and heeled the sorrel into a faster gait.

Since Shawcross and the other rustlers didn't seem to be coming after him, would they leave the area instead, he wondered. They didn't know he was a lawman; they thought he was another rustler. So they had no reason to be afraid that he would return with a posse to clean them out. Instead, they were more likely to stay where they were, determined to fight off any interlopers into their cattle-rustling operation.

Longarm hoped that would turn out to be the case. He

131

very much wanted another shot at Shawcross, Tobe, Darnell, and whatever the hell the other fella's name was.

First, though, he had to try to stop Sandra Nolan.

The sun rose higher as he rode. The heat of the day increased. Longarm sleeved sweat off his forehead. He came to the long barbed wire fence and the gate that marked the entrance to Prescott's range. From his visit the day before, he knew it was at least an hour's ride from here to Corpus Christi.

A glance at the sky told him the time was nearing noon.

Brooding about it wouldn't get him there any faster. He unlatched the gate, rode through, and swung it shut behind him. Then he sent the sorrel on north.

He had to fight the urge to kick the horse into a gallop. The animal had already run long and hard. If he faltered now and Longarm was left afoot, it would take him the rest of the day to walk into town. The *Night Wind* would be long gone by then, that was sure.

So he kept the sorrel moving at a steady pace. Finally, he saw the settlement ahead of him. Then and only then did he urge the horse into a run. It responded gallantly, carrying Longarm on into town.

He headed straight for the docks. He wasn't sure exactly what the *Night Wind* looked like, so his eyes searched the decks of all the vessels he passed for Sandra Nolan or Cappy Fitzgerald. When he came across a group of workers moving crates of cargo from a warehouse onto some wagons, he asked the man bossing the gang, "You know the ship *Night Wind*?"

"Sure, I know her," the man replied. "Miss Nolan's ship."

"Where's it tied up?" Longarm asked urgently.

"Nowhere anymore. She sailed an hour ago, outward bound for Vera Cruz."

Longarm's heart sank. He was too late. Sandra had sailed, and Bloody Tom Mahone was waiting out there somewhere for her.

But maybe there was still a chance, he told himself. He asked the dock worker, "Is there another ship leaving today?"

The man shook his head. "Ain't you heard, mister? Nobody's sailing much these days. They're all afraid of that damn pirate ship."

"Then there's no way to follow the *Night Wind* south?"

The man scratched his bristly jaw. "None that I can think of."

Longarm thought desperately for a moment, then asked, "Are there any towns between here and Mexico?" Someone somewhere else might be willing to take him out on a boat if he could get there in time.

"Well, there's Port Isabel, down by where the Rio Grande flows into the Gulf," the man said with a shrug. "That's about it."

Longarm had been to the town of Brownsville, a short distance inland along the Rio Grande, and he recalled nearby Port Isabel with its prominent lighthouse. "Much obliged," he said with a nod as he turned his horse toward the Nueces Hotel.

Catching up to Sandra Nolan would be a mighty long shot, but it was the only chance he had.

One thing was for damn sure: He couldn't afford to waste any time or spare any expense.

The clerk at the hotel stared at his disheveled appearance as he strode through the lobby and went up to his room. He had a spare Colt in his warbag. He got it out, loaded it, and slid it into the empty holster. He put the leather folder containing his badge and identification papers in his vest pocket, then filled his other pockets with extra ammunition for the Colt and the Winchester before heading downstairs again.

"I'll be gone a while," he said in passing to the clerk. "Hold on to my room."

"But, sir—"

Longarm paused long enough to show the clerk his bona fides. "I'm a federal lawman, and I ain't got time to argue about it. You'll get paid, don't worry."

With that, he was gone, hurrying down the street to the livery stable where he had left the sorrel. Ten minutes of furious activity netted him a string of three fast horses, along with a new saddle and tack. It was a double-cinched cowboy rig instead of the McClellan he preferred, but that was all right. He didn't have time to be picky.

It was about 150 miles to Port Isabel. He figured he could cover that distance in twelve hours if he switched out on the horses and rode at night. Given the fact that the *Night Wind* was carrying a full cargo, he thought it would take the ship that long, or perhaps even longer, to cover the same distance at sea. There was a chance he could hire a boat at Port Isabel to take him out and intercept Sandra's vessel.

The Gulf of Mexico was a big place. Even if he got there in time and found a boat, there was a chance he would miss the *Night Wind*. And it was possible that Mahone would strike before Sandra ever got that far. But Longarm had to take the chance, even though it would mean a long, hellish ride when he was already so exhausted that he felt on the verge of collapse.

He stopped at the café long enough to eat his first meal in over twelve hours and swig down a pot of coffee with it. The waitress was kind enough to lace the coffee with a healthy dollop of whiskey from the proprietor's private bottle. Then, fortified as best as he could be, Longarm collected his string of horses from the livery and started on the long trail south.

It was possible that word of his true identity as a deputy U.S. marshal would get around town, and Mort Shawcross might find out about it. If Shawcross heard the news and took off for the tall and uncut, that would be a shame, but Longarm could live with it. At least the rustling ring would be broken up that way. Trying to save Sandra and Cappy and the rest of the ship's crew was more important.

Longarm had made a lot of hard rides in his life. This one, down the coastal plain through the ranches belonging

134

to Hiram Prescott, Mifflin Kenedy, and Captain Richard King, ranked up there as one of the hardest. He had been riding or fighting almost constantly ever since he'd arrived in Corpus Christi, and by nightfall he hadn't had any sleep in thirty-six hours. He sometimes caught himself swaying in the saddle, eyes closed.

Whenever that happened, he snapped awake and forced himself back into a state of alertness. Luckily, the terrain was flat and the road was well marked. He had no trouble following it, even after darkness fell.

He kept the horses moving at a fast lope, riding one and leading the other two. Every ten miles or so, he stopped and switched the saddle to one of the other animals. From time to time he stopped and let them all rest for ten or fifteen minutes, though each such delay chafed at him.

But it was necessary to keep the horses fresh enough to keep moving. Even with these precautions, he could tell that the mounts were tiring.

However, the miles continued to flow behind him. By ten o'clock that night, he had come a long way, and he estimated that he was considerably closer to Port Isabel than he was to Corpus Christi.

He hadn't seen any lights for hours. This was empty land, fit for nothing but longhorns. Out here, under the vast sweep of sky and stars, a man could almost believe that he was alone upon the face of the earth, the sole human being in all of creation. It was a lonesome feeling, Longarm thought as he swung up into the saddle after resting the horses for a few minutes. It sure as hell was.

Later, he judged by the stars that it was after midnight, and when he pulled his turnip watch from his pocket and flipped it open to check it by the faint glow of starlight, he saw that his guess was right.

A short time after that, a bright light suddenly stabbed through the darkness in the distance ahead of him. It disappeared, but a moment later, it came again.

Longarm grinned wearily to himself. He knew the light

came from the Port Isabel lighthouse, with its mirrored Fresnel lens rotating around the oil-burning lamp. The light could be seen for about fifteen miles, so he knew he was at least that close. He stopped, moved the saddle onto the strongest of the three horses, and mounted up again, ready to make the last leg of the journey.

Port Isabel was a small settlement, little more than a fishing village except for the lighthouse that guided shipping through Brazos Santiago Pass into the mouth of the Rio Grande. The buildings, mostly of weathered wood, were dark at this time of night. Longarm headed for the lighthouse, knowing someone would be up and about there.

He had to pound on the lighthouse door for long minutes before an irritated voice called from inside, "Who the hell's out there? Don't you know what time it is, blast it?"

"U.S. marshal!" Longarm shouted back. "Open up! I'm here on official business!"

He heard footsteps clattering down the spiral staircase inside the lighthouse. The keeper yanked the door open and said, "Hold your horses! I got to come down more'n fifty feet o' stairs, you know." He was a tall man with stooped shoulders who peered owl-like at Longarm in the light of the lantern he held up in a bony hand. "Are you really a marshal?"

Longarm showed the man his badge.

"Well, what can I do for you?"

"I need a boat. I've got to go out on the Gulf."

"Tonight? That's crazy."

"It's a matter of life and death," Longarm said.

The lighthouse keeper rubbed his jaw. "You want a boat you can take out yourself, is that it?"

Longarm shook his head and said, "No, I'm not a sailor. I'll have to hire a skipper to go along with the boat."

"Well, you might find one o' these Mex fishermen

136

who'd be willin' to do it. If you got money. Lord knows they don't make a lot from fishin'.''

"I'll pay whatever's reasonable," Longarm said. Actually, he would pay more than that if he had to, but there was no point in admitting that. Henry was already liable to give him hell over his expenses on this case.

"All right, tell you what you do." The keeper stepped out of the lighthouse and pointed along the shore toward the pass. "Go down yonder about a quarter of a mile and you'll find a little shack that belongs to a fella name of Zapata. He's got a good boat and might be willin' to take you out."

"I'm much obliged." Longarm started to turn away.

"Somebody in trouble out on the Gulf?"

"I hope not yet," Longarm said over his shoulder.

He had no trouble finding the shack that the lighthouse keeper had mentioned. It was dark, but when he rattled the door in its frame with a fist, the wavering light of a candle filled the window.

"*Quien es?*" a man's voice asked from inside.

"Name's Custis Long. I'm a deputy United States marshal."

The door opened. The man inside wore a nightshirt and was stocky and a head shorter than Longarm, with thinning dark hair and a mustache. He had the candle in one hand, and an old shotgun was tucked under his other arm.

"I have broken no laws—" he began.

Longarm shook his head quickly. "No, I know that. I'm looking for somebody to take me out on the Gulf, and the fella up at the lighthouse said you might be interested in the job."

"Tomorrow, you mean?" Zapata asked.

"Nope, right now."

"But it is the middle of the night, señor."

"I know that. But it's mighty important that I get out there and meet a ship that's bound for Vera Cruz."

"You mean a cargo ship? Their lanes are several miles

137

offshore. I see them sometimes when I am fishing, though not as much these days."

Longarm didn't want to take the time to explain why the amount of shipping had dropped off recently. He said, "I'll sure make it worth your while, Señor Zapata."

The fisherman thought about it for a moment, then nodded. "*Sí*. I will do it. Let me get dressed."

"Can I leave my horses here? I reckon I've ridden 'em just about down to the nub."

"Of course. My cousin works on the boat with me and will be here early in the morning. I will leave him a note telling him to care for the *caballos*."

Longarm leaned against the wall and rested while he waited for Zapata. The fisherman took only a few minutes to get ready. Then he led Longarm down a path to the water, where a boat was tied up at a small pier. To Longarm's inexperienced eye, the two-masted craft looked rather small and rickety.

"Is this boat fast?" he asked.

Zapata smiled at him. "A fisherman seldom has the need to be swift, señor. But this boat is fast enough, and reliable, too. Please, come aboard."

Longarm stepped onto the deck while Zapata hurried around getting ready to cast off and raise the sails. Longarm helped as much as he could, though he would never make a sea dog. Finally, the fishing boat moved away from the pier, tacking into Brazos Santiago Pass because of the offshore breeze.

Zapata stood at the wheel, steering the craft with practiced ease. He said to Longarm, "When you appeared on my doorstep, señor, you looked very tired."

"Been a while since I had any sleep," Longarm admitted.

"There is room there on the deck to stretch out, and a blanket in that cabinet there. You should rest. It will be a good while before we reach the area where the big ships sail."

The offer was too tempting to resist. Longarm took the

blanket from the cabinet and made a pallet on the deck. The blanket smelled of fish and the deck was hard . . .

But as he stretched out, it felt as good to Longarm as a feather bed, and he was asleep as soon as he closed his eyes.

Chapter 18

Longarm let out a groan as he forced his eyes open. He winced as sunlight struck them.

Then, as awareness soaked into his sleep-stunned brain, he sat bolt upright and looked around wildly.

The sun was a hand's span above the eastern horizon. Longarm lurched to his knees and grasped the fishing boat's gunwale as he stared at the fiery orb. It was well after dawn, and he had slept much longer than he'd intended to.

"Ah, señor, you are awake."

When he heard Zapata's voice, Longarm pushed himself to his feet and turned angrily toward the fisherman. "Damn it, why'd you let me sleep so long?"

"You were tired," Zapata said simply.

Longarm bit back a curse. What had happened to Sandra and the *Night Wind*? Had the ship sailed past in the darkness? Or had the vessel never even made it this far?

"I was hoping to intercept that ship—" Longarm began.

"I know, señor. We are in the shipping lanes. We have been sailing back and forth in them for several hours. No ship has gone past us."

Longarm felt like groaning again, this time from despair. Either they had missed the *Night Wind* because the

140

ship had not followed its usual course, or Bloody Tom Mahone had already sunk it. Those seemed like the only possible answers.

Zapata was still at the wheel. He reached down to the deck beside him and picked up an earthenware jug with a cork stopper in its neck. As he extended the jug toward Longarm, he said, "Here, Marshal. An eye-opener."

Longarm thought about growling that he didn't want a drink, but then he took the jug, pulled the cork, and tilted it to his mouth. The fiery tequila inside made him gasp as it blazed through his mouth and gullet. But it did clear some of the cobwebs from his brain, as he'd hoped.

He wiped the back of his free hand across his mouth and then asked, "Any chance that ship slipped past us in the dark?"

"There is always a chance, señor," Zapata replied with a shrug, "but I honestly do not believe this happened."

"Damn it," Longarm muttered. It was looking more and more as if some misfortune—perhaps a deadly one—had befallen the ship before it got this far down the coast.

"Señor . . . was there maybe a woman on this ship you seek?"

"Yeah. How'd you know that?"

Zapata shrugged again. "The French have a saying— *cherchez la femme*. Seek the woman. Always the explanation involves a señorita or a señora."

Longarm's eyes narrowed. "You weren't always a fisherman, were you, old son?"

"Once I taught the natural and physical sciences at the university in Mexico City. Now I fish. It is a much more pleasant life."

Despite his worry over Sandra's fate, Longarm chuckled. "There are times I wouldn't mind spending the rest of my days sitting on the bank of a mountain stream with a fishing pole in my hand. I reckon I know what you mean, Señor Zapata."

The fisherman used his foot to nudge a sack on the deck. "There are tortillas. Help yourself, Marshal."

Longarm ate some tortillas, washing them down with another swig of the tequila. His eyes searched the waves as he ate, looking for some sign of the *Night Wind*. They were out of sight of land, so there was nothing to see except the rolling, blue-green sea and the blue, cloud-dotted sky.

Suddenly, Longarm thought he saw a flash of white in the distance. He couldn't tell for sure, but he thought it might be the sail of a ship. Since he was sort of turned around on where they were, he pointed and asked Zapata, "Is that north?"

The fisherman nodded. "Yes. And I see it, too, señor. It is a ship."

Longarm felt a sense of relief wash through him. There was no guarantee that the vessel coming toward them was Sandra's, but until he found out otherwise, he was going to hope that it was.

Zapata swung the fishing boat around on a course that would intercept that of the larger vessel. As the ship came closer, Longarm was able to make out the three masts with their separate sets of sails.

"You wouldn't happen to have a pair of field glasses on board, would you?"

Zapata handed him a telescope. "Try this spyglass."

Longarm pulled the telescope out to its full length and squinted through the lens. The ship seemed to leap at his eye when he found it again. He spotted a white-bearded figure scurrying around on deck and thought it was Cappy Fitzgerald. When he lifted the spyglass to the bridge, he saw a slim figure with long dark hair blowing in the wind of the ship's passage through the water.

Longarm dragged in a deep breath. That was Sandra Nolan, and she was all right. His long ride down the coast had been a success.

"Can we get in front of 'em?" he asked as he lowered the spyglass.

"*Sí*, if the wind holds, and I believe it will."

The fishing boat continued its wallowing course

142

through the waves. Longarm began to feel a little queasy. Most of the time he had a cast-iron stomach, and when he had been on ships before, he seldom got seasick. But he was worn down now, and the tequila on an empty stomach probably hadn't been a good idea, either.

He swallowed hard, determined not to get sick now that he had almost accomplished his objective. As the *Night Wind* came closer, he started to feel better. He waved his arms over his head, wondering if anyone on board the larger vessel had seen the fishing boat.

The crew began to strike some of the sails. The ship slowed. Longarm knew they had seen him. He turned to Zapata and asked, "Can you come alongside her?"

"Of course."

The fisherman skillfully maneuvered his craft until it was sailing alongside the larger vessel. The *Night Wind* was more than twice as tall as the little fishing boat. As Longarm looked up, he saw a rope ladder tossed over the side.

"I'm much obliged, señor," he said as he shook hands with Zapata. He gave a wad of greenbacks to the fisherman. "If you need more than that, write to Chief Marshal Billy Vail in Denver, and he'll see to it that you're paid."

"This is fine, Marshal," Zapata said with a smile as he tucked away the money. "You are going on the ship now?"

"That's right. You did a fine job, a mighty fine job."

"*Gracias, señor*. And *vaya con Dios*."

Longarm balanced himself carefully on the gunwale, holding on to one of the lines as he did so, and when the waves brought the two vessels almost together, he leaned out and reached for the rope ladder. Grasping it firmly, he swung over to the *Night Wind* and began to climb.

Sandra Nolan and Cappy Fitzgerald, both of them with incredulous stares on their faces, were waiting for him at the top. Cappy helped Longarm over the railing onto the deck.

143

"Custis, what in the name of all that's holy are you doing here?" Sandra demanded.

Longarm grinned. "I came to see you, of course." The grin vanished, to be replaced by a grim expression. "I came to warn you. You're sailing into a trap. Bloody Tom Mahone intends to sink this ship."

"What?" Cappy yelped. "But . . . but I thought you said there wasn't no such thing as ghosts!"

"There's not, and the fella I'm talking about ain't really Bloody Tom Mahone. He's flesh and blood, and I've got a hunch he's really Mauler Larribee."

"Larribee," Sandra breathed. "Yes, he's capable of being a pirate. But I still don't understand any of this."

Longarm glanced around at the crew. Many of them were middle-aged or older, like Cappy, and they were listening intently while trying to appear not to do so. Longarm said, "Why don't we go to your cabin, and I'll explain the whole thing."

Sandra hesitated, but then she nodded and said, "All right. Cappy, the bridge is yours."

"Aye, aye, Cap'n," the old-timer said. "But when you find out what's goin' on here, tell me, why don't you, 'cause I'm almighty confused."

"Turn back?" Sandra said when Longarm had explained everything that had happened, including his true identity as a federal lawman. "I can't do that."

"You don't have any choice. I ain't sure why Mahone, or Larribee, or whoever he really is, ain't hit you before now, but he's bound and determined not to let you make it to Vera Cruz."

"I don't care. If I don't complete this voyage and deliver our cargo, I won't be able to save the ship. You're right, Custis, I don't have any choice. I have to go on."

"If you won't go back to Corpus, at least put in at Port Isabel and stay there for a few days while I try to sort things out and get my hands on Larribee. Then you can go on to Vera Cruz."

"Impossible," she snapped. "That's too much of a delay. Besides, why would Larribee want to sink this ship? According to what you told me, he's a rustler!"

Longarm gritted his teeth for a second before answering, "He's got more than one iron in the fire. Yeah, he's working with Shawcross to loot Hiram Prescott's herd, but at the same time he's trying to ruin shipping up and down the Gulf Coast."

"Why?"

Longarm shook his head. "Beats the hell out of me. Maybe he figures that once all the other ships have given up, he'll control things in this part of the country. He's made a damned good start on it."

"Well, maybe you're right," Sandra admitted. "But I still can't turn back. We'll just have to take our chances."

"I'll have to take 'em with you, then."

"We could head for the mainland long enough to put you ashore," Sandra offered. "We're already a little south of Port Isabel, but there are several fishing villages along the coast. Maybe you could buy a horse or something."

Longarm shook his head. "Nope, I'll stay with you."

Sandra sat down on the edge of the bunk. "That's up to you, Custis. I'll admit, though, I wouldn't mind having your company for the rest of the voyage. Cappy's an old dear, but I've heard all of his stories at least a dozen times."

Longarm summoned up a grin. "All right, then, it's settled. We sail on to Vera Cruz."

"We should be there in about three days," Sandra said.

"I expected you to be further along than you were. I was afraid I'd missed you."

"We had trouble with one of the sails, and that slowed us down," she explained. "But we're making good speed now, and I don't foresee any more problems."

"Except maybe pirates," Longarm pointed out dryly.

"Yes," she agreed, "except maybe pirates."

• • •

But as the *Night Wind* continued sailing southward along the coast, there was no sign of Bloody Tom Mahone's ebony-sailed ship. Longarm might have wondered if he had imagined the whole thing, if he hadn't been too hard-headed to know that wasn't the case. He had witnessed the meeting between Shawcross and the pirate, whoever that was masquerading as Mahone.

For some unknown reason, though, Mahone had not attacked Sandra's ship as planned. Longarm was certainly prepared to accept a little luck.

Sailing as a passenger on a vessel like this was a lot different than being shanghaied into serving on its crew, he thought as he stood at the railing and watched the sea race past. Cappy handled the crew and the ship and did a fine job. He was captain in everything but name, as Sandra had planned, and he responded well to the responsibility. Maybe he had finally put the tragedy and guilt behind him. Longarm hoped so, because he liked the old-timer.

Right on schedule, the *Night Wind* sailed into the big harbor at Vera Cruz. The cargo was unloaded, and sweating stevedores loaded a new cargo of bananas and sugarcane that the ship would carry back to Corpus Christi. That night, except for a few men left on board to stand watch, the crew was allowed to go ashore for some recreation.

Cappy laughed and rubbed his hands together in anticipation as he and Longarm and Sandra stood on deck by the gangplank. His hair was slicked back and he smelled of bay rum. "It's amazin' how much younger those old coots get whenever there's liquor and señoritas waitin' for 'em." He grinned at Longarm. "Sure you don't want to come with us?"

"No, you go ahead and have a good time," Longarm told him.

"Just keep track of the men and get them all back here in one piece," Sandra added. "I want to sail as early as possible tomorrow."

146

"Aye, aye, Cap'n." Cappy sketched a salute and set off down the gangplank, whistling as he went.

"What are your plans for the evening, Custis, since you're not going ashore?" Sandra asked.

"I ain't really given it much thought."

"Then why don't you have dinner with me in my cabin?"

Longarm grinned at her. "I can't think of one good reason in the world not to."

Chapter 19

Sandra had the ship's cook, an elderly seaman named Davis, prepare the meal. The food started as simple shipboard fare, salted beef and potatoes, but Davis had gone ashore and bought enough peppers and spices in Vera Cruz's market to make the dinner different and delicious. Davis brought back a bottle of sangria, too.

"I reckon you're just about the prettiest ship's captain I ever saw," Longarm told Sandra as they sat at the table in her cabin. The maps and charts that were usually scattered on the table had been cleared away and replaced with a linen tablecloth and nice china.

She wore a green dress that left her shoulders mostly bare and went well with her brown eyes. Smiling at the compliment he had given her, she asked, "What about that riverboat woman up in Alaska?"

"Well, she was mighty pretty, too," Longarm said. "I'd sure hate to have to choose between the two of you."

"I suppose it's a good thing, then, that we're thousands of miles apart."

"That could be true," Longarm said diplomatically.

When they had finished eating, Sandra poured more sangria in their glasses. She twirled it around and studied Longarm over the rim of her glass.

"I've been thinking about that ride you made down the

coast," she said. "That must have almost killed you."

He shrugged. "I'm sure it was a lot harder on the horses."

"Still, you'd fought with those rustlers and then been captured by them and escaped . . . You must have been exhausted."

"I was feeling a mite peaked by the time I got to Port Isabel," Longarm admitted. "But I'm all better now. Reckon all this sea air was good for me."

She laughed. "You're a good sailor . . . for a landlubber."

"Well, I got to admit, I'm just as happy not to be bouncing around on those waves. It's a mighty pleasant evening."

"Yes," Sandra said softly. "It is."

The two portholes in the cabin were open, letting in the tropical breezes and the soft murmur of sounds from the docks along the harbor, along with the gentle lapping of the water. The light of day had faded from the sky. The cabin was illuminated by the glow from a lamp that was attached to the wall, a lamp that Sandra turned down as she stood up from the table.

She held out her glass toward Longarm. "Drink to the sea with me, Custis?"

He got to his feet and went over to her. "To the sea," he said as he lightly clinked his glass against hers.

They drank, and her eyes never left his as they did. When the glasses were empty, Longarm took both of them and set them on the table. He turned back to Sandra and moved toward her. She didn't retreat. She reached up, slipped her arms around his neck, and pulled his head down so that his mouth met hers.

Longarm took her into his arms as he kissed her, holding her around the waist. Her mouth was warm and eager, and her body trembled slightly with readiness as she molded herself against him. His tongue stroked her lips. They parted without hesitation, inviting him to explore the hot, wet sweetness of her mouth.

His shaft was hard, prodding the softness of her belly through their clothing. Longarm moved a hand up her side and slipped it between them to cup the firm flesh of her breast. She caught at the back of his neck and arched her pelvis against him as he strummed the hard nubbin of her nipple through her dress.

She broke the kiss and whispered, "Undress me, Custis."

Longarm was glad to oblige.

She went to work on his clothes as he started unfastening and unsnapping hers, and within a few minutes they had stripped each other. Sandra was beautiful. Her skin was like honey in the soft glow of the lamp. Her breasts weren't overly large, but they rode high and firm on her chest and had large, dark brown nipples. She was exquisitely shaped, curving in and out in the classic female form. The triangle of brown hair between her legs seemed to be inviting Longarm to stroke it, so he did, running his fingers through the soft, fine-spun strands.

She caught hold of his hand and pressed it against her, rubbing it up and down on her mound. Her eyes closed and she sighed in delight. Longarm moved his hand lower, probed with a finger, and found the slick heat of her opening. She gasped and parted her thighs a little as he slipped the finger inside her.

Longarm moved his finger in and out. She was tight, the walls of her sex clasping his finger like heated butter. It was going to feel even better when he filled her with his manhood, which by now was as stiff as a bar of iron.

The long, thick pole of flesh throbbed as Sandra closed her hands around it. "Custis, I want you inside me!" she said urgently as she tugged him toward the bunk.

Longarm went with her. As she sprawled on her back and spread her legs, he moved between her thighs and poised there on his knees. There was no need for delay. Droplets of dew already sparkled on the folds of flesh that marked the entrance to her core. The passion that had sprung up between them at their first touch was deep and strong, and their need for each other was immediate. Longarm brought the head of his shaft to her opening and dipped it in the wetness.

Then with a thrust of his hips he surged into her, sheathing himself completely and filling her to the brim.

It felt every bit as good as he had thought it would. Sensations cascaded through him as Sandra gave a soft cry and tossed her head back and forth on the pillow. Her buttocks came off the bunk as she met his thrust with one of her own. His hips began to pump back and forth as he drove in and out of her.

He started off as slow as he could, pausing between some of the strokes to relish the feeling of being as deep inside her as he could go. But he had to pick up the pace, and within moments both of them were panting and gasping and surging at each other.

With the need between them so high, the culmination could not be put off for long. Longarm watched Sandra's breasts bouncing with each thrust and saw the way the fires grew in her heavy-lidded eyes. He slipped his hands underneath her rump and pulled her up to him as he penetrated deeper and deeper. He felt his climax boiling up and could do nothing to stop it.

With a groan, he exploded inside her, pouring out his seed in one throbbing, white-hot jet after another. Sandra shuddered and clutched at him and shook from the force of her own climax. Both of them reached the peak together; then, wrapped in each other's arms, they started the long, slow, sweet slide down the other side.

The bunk wasn't big enough for both of them to lie side by side, so after a moment Sandra said, "Custis, that was absolutely wonderful, but you have to get off now."

He pushed himself up. He was just starting to catch his breath, and his pulse still hammered inside his skull. "Sorry," he said. "Reckon I was just about crushing you."

"Not really." She grinned up at him. "To tell you the truth, it felt good to have you on top of me. But we have to change places."

"Why?"

Her grin got to be more wicked. "Because *I* want to be on top next time," she said.

Later that night, Longarm stood up on deck, his hands on the railing, and looked out to sea. He enjoyed the warm Gulf breeze blowing in his face. It smelled clean and good.

Down below in the captain's cabin, Sandra was asleep. Longarm had waited until she was breathing deeply and regularly before pulling on his pants and shirt and slipping out of the cabin to come up on deck. All his aches and pains were gone, healed by three days on the *Night Wind*.

He took a cheroot from his pocket and set fire to it. As he tossed the lucifer over the side into the water, he heard a footstep behind him on the deck and turned to see Cappy Fitzgerald.

Cappy grinned and moved up to the railing beside Longarm. "How was your dinner?" the old-timer asked.

"Just fine. How was your shore leave?"

Cappy sighed. "Over too soon, for me and the pretty little señorita I was with. But I get a mite restless if I have dry land under my feet for too long. I get to missin' the feel of a ship's deck."

"It was a good thing you did, helping Sandra like that. Getting her a crew and taking charge of everything."

"Sandy's like my own daughter, I reckon," Cappy said wistfully. "I never had no kids of my own. Never could stay hitched to one woman long enough. It takes a special kind o' gal to put up with a seafarin' man."

"I expect it does," Longarm agreed. He took a puff on the cheroot, blew a smoke ring that drifted out over the water for a second before the persistent breeze pulled it apart. "We'll be ready to sail first thing in the morning?"

"Damn right."

"I didn't say anything about it to Sandra, but I don't reckon we're out of the woods yet," Longarm said slowly. "I know that so-called pirate wanted to sink this ship. Just because he didn't try anything on the way down here doesn't mean he won't on the way back."

Cappy tugged at his beard worriedly. "I know it. Don't know a damn thing in the world we can do about it, though, except sail on and hope for the best."

That was true of just about everything in life, Longarm reflected as he nodded and looked out over the black waters of the Gulf.

The crewmen looked bleary-eyed and tired the next morning, but somehow they seemed younger than before, as if the night in Vera Cruz had revitalized them somehow. Longarm overheard one of the old-timers telling another, "When we get back to Corpus, I think I'm gonna sign on for another voyage. It's hard to sit on the land when the sea's in your blood."

Longarm supposed he could understand that feeling, even though he didn't share it. He felt the same way about the West. He could never go back east to stay. He would miss the mountains and the prairies and the big sky too much to ever do that.

Following Cappy's brisk commands, the crew got ready to cast off, and soon the *Night Wind* sailed out of the harbor and headed north toward Corpus Christi.

The first three days of the voyage truly were idyllic: clear blue skies, a fair wind, and nothing between them and home except miles of beautiful blue-green sea. The nights weren't bad, either. With all the crew aboard, Sandra hadn't felt like making love again, but Longarm dined with her every evening and then stretched out in a hammock strung up on the stern. He smoked cheroots and looked up at the stars and swapped yarns—some true, some not—with Cappy and some of the other sailors.

As peaceful as things were, though, worry still lurked in the back of Longarm's mind. He hadn't forgotten how serious Bloody Tom Mahone had sounded when he declared that he intended to sink the *Night Wind*.

They passed Port Isabel and were off the Texas coast

again. Sandra ordered Cappy to alter their course slightly, so that they were in sight of Padre Island as they sailed north. Longarm found himself standing at the railing with her that day, watching as the long, low line of tan and brown that marked the barrier island drifted past about a mile to port. The sky had turned cloudy, and the wind was whipping up a little harder than usual.

"Did you know there are cattle out there?" Sandra asked. "Most of them run wild now, but once there was a ranch on the island, founded by a Spanish priest."

Longarm had heard the story of how Padre Island got its name, but he enjoyed listening to Sandra, so he let her carry on. She talked about how Spanish explorers had come here more than three hundred years earlier, the first Europeans to set foot on this part of the North American continent.

"This is where civilization got its first foothold in Texas," she said as she pushed back thick brown hair that the wind had blown into her face. "Imagine that."

Longarm nodded. "Yep. And some folks say things have been going downhill ever since."

She grinned at him. "Don't you like civilization, Custis? I would think that as a marshal, you'd have to be on the side of law and order."

"Oh, I am," he said. "You got to have civilization— law and order and everything that goes with it—to make a wild land a fit place for ordinary folks to live. But I reckon I can see how the Indians feel about it, and the explorers and such-like who saw the Western lands when they weren't tamed. They played their part, but now their time is over."

"Just like the pirates."

Longarm nodded. "That's right. Somebody can dress up like Bloody Tom Mahone to try to scare folks, but he's just playacting. He ain't the real thing and never can be, because those days are gone."

"These new pirates are still dangerous, though."

"They sure are. Probably just as dangerous as the first ones."

At that moment, the sailor on lookout duty in the crow's nest bellowed down, "Sail ho!"

Sandra looked up, saw which way the man was pointing, and hurried across the deck to the starboard rail. Longarm went with her.

He felt his pulse increase as he stared out across the waves at the vessel cutting toward them off the starboard bow. Instead of the usual white sails, it was rigged with black ones.

"My God," Sandra breathed. "It's—"

"Mahone," Longarm finished for her. "Or rather, Mauler Larribee, more than likely."

Sandra turned her head and shouted up to the bridge, where Cappy Fitzgerald had the wheel. "Cappy! Get us closer to land!"

"Aye, Sandy!" Cappy called back. He was already spinning the big wheel. He had seen the approaching ship, too.

Sandra grasped the railing tightly. "I thought we were going to be lucky enough to avoid him."

"We'll have to try to fight them off," Longarm said. "How are you fixed for arms?"

"We have several Winchesters on board, but only one cannon. It's a four-inch gun."

Longarm nodded. That wasn't much with which to fight off an attack by pirates, but it would have to do. He put a hand on Sandra's shoulder and said, "Better get below. This is the sort of job I'm better suited to handle."

"But I'm the captain!" she protested. Her eyes blazed with an angry light. "I'm not going to go cower in my cabin."

Longarm saw that it would be futile to argue with her. "Then go up on the bridge with Cappy. Do you have a pistol?"

She shook her head.

He drew his Colt from the cross-draw rig and pressed

the weapon into her hands. "Take this, then. I'll use one of the Winchesters."

"All right. Be careful, Custis."

Longarm thought it was a mite late for that, but he didn't say so. Instead he just grinned reassuringly at her and replied, "You, too."

As she went to the bridge, Sandra ordered one of the sailors to go below and break open the arms locker. Longarm went with the man and took the first Winchester out of the locker, loading it from a box of cartridges. He dropped more cartridges into his pocket, then supervised the passing out of the rest of the rifles and had the men who were armed with them line up along the starboard rail. In the meantime, the gun crew that manned the cannon rolled the four-inch gun across the deck and locked it down in the forward gun port.

Longarm watched the black-sailed ship come closer. The ebony sails were full of wind and the vessel sped along gracefully through the water, which was growing choppier.

But the *Night Wind* was making a good run for the shore. Longarm glanced over his shoulder and saw that the sandy dunes of Padre Island were drawing steadily closer.

The island offered no real protection from the pirates, but at least in shallower water the crew would stand a better chance of surviving if they had to abandon ship.

Longarm went up to the bridge to join Sandra and Cappy. Sandra said to the old-timer, "We can't outrun them, can we?"

Cappy shook his head. "Nope, I don't reckon we can. They've got more sail than we do, and they're lighter in the water. We're gonna have to fight 'em." He looked up at the sky, which was growing darker. "Almost wish that squall that's brewin' up would go ahead and break. Might make it easier to slip away if those damned pirates had something else to worry about."

Thunder rumbled in the distance, but Longarm figured

the storm was too far away to have an effect on the up-coming battle. The next moment there was a loud boom, but it didn't come from the thunder.

Instead, it was a cannon firing on the deck of Bloody Tom Mahone's ship, and as Longarm brought the Winchester to his shoulder he saw the splash just off the starboard bow of the *Night Wind* where the shot struck.

The pirates had called the turn and opened the ball. The deadly dance had begun.

Chapter 20

Longarm sighted grimly over the rifle barrel. He couldn't see very many men moving around on the deck of the black-sailed ship. But when one of the pirates revealed himself, Longarm fired, feeling the familiar kick of the Winchester against his shoulder.

As far as he could tell, he didn't hit a damned thing.

Of course, it was difficult aiming when the waves made the deck of the *Night Wind* rise and fall underneath him. The pirate ship was bobbing up and down, too. Longarm worked the Winchester's lever, jacking another cartridge into the chamber, and waited for a chance to shoot again.

"Fire at will!" Sandra called down to the crewmen manning the cannon. A moment later the four-incher roared. Longarm saw the splash as the ball struck the water well short of the pirate ship.

Longarm grimaced. He had a feeling that Mahone's gunners would get the range before the ones on the *Night Wind* did.

"Aim for the gun ports!" he shouted to the riflemen along the railing. Their best chance was to keep those boys hopping for cover so that they couldn't line up a shot that would cripple the cargo ship.

He did his part, peppering the other vessel with bullets. It was close enough now so that he could see splinters fly as the result of some of his shots. He was even rewarded by the sight of one of the pirates falling as a slug from Longarm's gun tore through him.

A haze of powder smoke drifted over the deck. Cannons on both vessels roared again. A heavy cannonball tore through the *Night Wind*'s rigging but missed the masts.

Longarm felt a sudden shiver go through the ship as a ball struck it. Behind him, Sandra cried out as if the impact caused her physical pain and Cappy gave vent to a bitter curse. "We've been holed!" the old-timer cried.

"Keep heading for shore!" Sandra ordered. She came to the railing beside Longarm and lifted the pistol in her hand, but he pushed her arm down before she could fire.

"The range is too great for a handgun," he told her. "Save your bullets for the close fighting. You're liable to need 'em."

He was no sea dog, but even he could feel the way the ship had begun to wallow. It was taking on water, no doubt about that. But there would be crewmen below, operating the pumps in an effort to keep the *Night Wind* afloat.

Longarm turned his head to look toward Padre Island. The shore was no more than half a mile away now. Their best hope was to run the vessel aground, fight off the pirates, and then repair the damage. It was a long shot, but the only chance they had.

In the meantime, the black-sailed ship continued to close in, and the storm was growing stronger, too. The clouds were almost as black as the sails on the pirate ship. The wind lashed at Longarm's face, and he felt the occasional sting of a drop of rain.

"Damn you!" Cappy shouted over the howl of the wind. "Damn you to hell!"

Longarm glanced at the old man and saw to his surprise that Cappy wasn't looking at the pirates. His hands were curled into claws that tightly gripped the wheel, and he had his head thrown back as he shouted curses at the sky.

Longarm remembered the story Sandra had told him about how Cappy had lost his ship in a storm. He realized that the old-timer was raging not at a human foe, but at the fates that had sent him sailing into another such squall. Or perhaps in his mind he had mixed up the two and thought he was cursing the very storm that had cost him his ship, his crew, and his self-respect.

Either way, it didn't really matter. What was important was that the black-sailed ship was closing in. Powder smoke spurted as the pirates opened fire with rifles and handguns. Bullets whined through the air. Men on both ships fell, blood welling from their wounds.

One of the pirates spun a grappling hook attached to a sturdy rope over his head. He was about to cast it toward the *Night Wind* when Longarm shot him, the bullet driving him back off his feet. But a second later another man took his place, and the grappling hook flew through the air and caught over the cargo ship's railing. More lines were thrown across. The waves brought the vessels inexorably closer together until mere feet separated them.

"We're bein' boarded!" one of the crewmen yelled as a couple of pirates leaped across that gap and landed on the deck of the *Night Wind*. Both had pistols, and they opened fire. Longarm spun and chopped down one of them with a bullet from the Winchester, but not before the pirate had wounded a couple of the crew.

More pirates followed, until the deck of the cargo ship was filled with knots of men desperately struggling for their lives. Longarm couldn't fire into the fracas because the chances were too great that he would hit one of Sandra's men. Instead he leaped down among them and joined the fight.

He caved in the back of a pirate's skull with a stroke of the rifle butt. Before he could strike again, another pirate snapped a shot at him. The bullet barely clipped the top of his left shoulder, but the impact was still great enough to spin him halfway around and drop him to one knee. A man fell against him, spouting blood from a slashed throat, and knocked Longarm to the deck.

From there he saw Bloody Tom Mahone leap from the pirate ship to the *Night Wind* and wade into the melee with that old-fashioned cutlass. Men shrieked and fell as they felt the deadly kiss of that cold steel, wielded with bloodthirsty viciousness by the huge, bearded man.

Longarm had dropped the Winchester when he was knocked down. He reached for it, hoping for a shot at Mahone. Before he could get his hands on the rifle, though, Mahone leaped to the bridge and lunged toward Sandra. She lifted the pistol in her hand and fired at him.

Incredibly, the bullets didn't seem to have much effect on Mahone. He kept coming toward her, staggering a little under the impact but not falling. He swung the cutlass.

Suddenly, Cappy Fitzgerald was between Mahone and Sandra. Longarm's eyes widened in horror and rage as he saw the blade bite deep into Cappy's chest. Somehow, the old man found the strength to stay on his feet. He grappled with the much larger man as he shouted, "Sandy! Get outta here!"

Despite the old man's plea, Sandra might have remained rooted to the spot on the bridge if a particularly large wave had not lifted the ship at that moment. She lost her balance and went backward toward the railing. With a startled cry, she hit it, flipped in the air, and was gone over backward into the Gulf, vanishing in the wink of an eye.

Longarm surged to his feet, shouting incoherently in rage, and started toward the bridge. He had taken only a couple of steps, though, when something smashed into the back of his head and drove him off his feet. He felt himself sliding on the blood-slick deck as it tilted again, but he couldn't stop.

He shot over the side and plummeted toward the fierce waves below.

• • •

161

He figured he never really lost consciousness. If he had been out cold, he would have slipped under the surface and drowned right away. But he had been stunned enough by the blow to the head so that he wasn't really aware of anything for a while, even though he had kicked off his boots and kept himself afloat by treading water.

He didn't know where the storm had carried him, but the *Night Wind* was gone and so was the black-sailed ship commanded by the ghost of Bloody Tom Mahone. Maybe Mahone really *was* a ghost. He had shrugged off those bullets like he didn't really exist.

But he was real enough to have plunged his cutlass into the chest of Cappy Fitzgerald, Longarm thought bitterly. And he suddenly had an idea why the shots from Sandra's gun hadn't stopped Mahone. The problem would be living long enough to do anything about that idea.

He almost slipped under a few times, and he knew he couldn't continue to tread water indefinitely. So he started swimming, following a seagull that flew overhead, in hopes that the bird was heading for Padre Island. The island couldn't be too far away, Longarm told himself. He was just too low in the water to see it.

Then the sleek gray fin of a shark started following him, and he knew he wasn't going to make it. He kept swimming anyway, just too damned stubborn to give up.

At first he thought he was imagining the voice calling his name. But then it grew louder, and when he looked up and blinked water out of his eyes, he saw Sandra Nolan crouched on a piece of floating wreckage, holding out a hand toward him.

She was soaked to the skin and utterly bedraggled, but she looked like an angel to Longarm. He began to stroke harder, swimming for his life toward her. He didn't look back. If the shark was gaining on him, he didn't want to know about it.

He reached up, grasped Sandra's wrist, and she hauled back hard as she caught hold of his wrist. As he came up out of the water and sprawled onto the wreckage, he sensed something huge passing right below him. The chunk of debris rocked in the water as the shark bumped it. Longarm and Sandra both flattened out and hung on, hoping the makeshift raft wouldn't tip over.

The wreckage stabilized after a moment. Panting, Longarm looked for the shark's fin and saw it moving away from them. He gave a hollow laugh.

"He's not going to take the trouble to come after us," Sandra said, her voice weak with relief. "He's looking for an easier meal."

"That's fine . . . with me," Longarm said. He reached over and grasped Sandra's hand. "Are you all right?"

She nodded. "Just wet and scared. And mad. The *Night Wind* is gone."

"The crew?"

"All dead. Even Cappy." Tears welled from her eyes and she sounded hollow with grief. "That bastard Mahone stabbed him."

"I saw that much. And then you went overboard."

She nodded. "I managed to stay afloat. I saw Mahone's men murder my whole crew. Then they didn't even bother to steal the cargo. They just went back to their ship, pulled away, and blew the *Night Wind* to pieces with their cannons." She patted the debris under them. "This is a piece of the hull."

Longarm had already figured that out. The chunk of wood was barely large enough for both of them to lie on it. But it would serve to save their lives as long as no more hungry sharks came around.

He pushed himself up on his elbows and looked ahead of them. Now he could see Padre Island. The waves carried them steadily toward the shore, which was only a few hundred yards away.

A short time later, the debris washed up on the beach, bringing Longarm and Sandra with it. They staggered off the wreckage and fell onto the sand, breathing heavily. It began to rain, cold hard drops that slashed down from the leaden skies. Longarm didn't mind. But after a while, as the tide began to creep up along their legs, they got up and stumbled farther inland, dragging the piece of the *Night Wind*'s hull with them. They went several hundred yards before collapsing.

Later, Longarm wasn't sure if he passed out or just fell asleep, but it was night when he came awake again. He sat up, alarmed for a moment until he looked around and saw Sandra stretched out beside him. Relaxing a little, he took several deep breaths and tried to clear his mind.

They were out of immediate danger, but they were still in a bad fix, he thought as he looked up at the millions of stars twinkling overhead. The sky was clear. The storm had moved on. There was that to be thankful for, anyway.

It might have been better if it had still been raining, though. At least then he could have tried to rig something to catch the rainwater. As it was, he and Sandra had nothing to drink. The water in the Laguna Madre wasn't quite as salty as the Gulf, but it wasn't fit to drink. They could walk all the way back up Padre Island to Corpus Christi, but they would be dead of thirst before they got there. He wasn't sure how far it was to Port Isabel, but it seemed unlikely they could reach that settlement, either.

It had rained hard that afternoon. Maybe there were still some puddles around. The water would be muddy, but it would be better than nothing. He got to his feet and began to search.

He found a small puddle, cupped some of the water in his hands, and tasted it. It was palatable enough, only a little salty. He was about to go back and get Sandra when he heard her calling his name frantically.

Longarm hurried back to the spot where he had left her. She was running around aimlessly. He caught hold of her shoulders and said, "It's all right, Sandra. I'm right here. I was just looking for water."

She threw her arms around his neck and hugged him, trembling as she did so. "Oh, Custis, I thought you were dead. I was afraid I had just imagined you being with me."

"I'm here," he told her again. "And I ain't going anywhere without you."

He led her back to the puddle. In the moonlight, they dropped to their knees beside it and used their hands to scoop out a hole. More water trickled into it. There wasn't enough to really satisfy them, but they felt better after they drank.

"What are we going to do?" Sandra asked as she sat back on her heels.

"I've been thinking about that. Ain't likely anybody's going to come along and rescue us, so we'll have to walk out of here."

"We can't walk up Padre Island. We'd die of thirst."

Longarm nodded. "That's right. So we've got to get back to the mainland. That means getting across the Laguna Madre somehow. It's mighty shallow in a lot of places, so I'm hoping we can walk across it."

"And if we come to a place where the water is too deep to wade through it, we can use that piece of hull as a raft again," Sandra said, and Longarm was glad to hear the hope come back into her voice. "I think we could do it, Custis."

"Once we get to the mainland, there ought to be enough fresh water around to keep us going. Maybe I can rig a snare, catch us a rabbit or two. Of course, we may have to eat 'em raw, but . . ."

"It's better than dying," Sandra declared. "And we have to stay alive. We just have to." Her voice hardened even more. "Otherwise we'll never be able to even the score with Bloody Tom Mahone."

Chapter 21

They were able to hike across Padre Island during the night and reached the shore of the lagoon before dawn. Longarm knew the inland waterway was eight or ten miles wide. It would probably take them all day to get across.

And once they got out into the lagoon and lost sight of Padre Island, there would be no landmarks until they got close enough to the mainland to see it. They would have to be very careful not to get turned around and start walking in the wrong direction.

They looked at each other as the sun rose. Their wet clothes had dried during the night, but they were still dirty and disheveled.

"Well," Sandra said, "do we give it a try?"

"Might as well," Longarm said, trying to keep his voice light. "I didn't have any other plans for today, anyway."

He took off his belt and fed it through a hole in the piece of wreckage, then tied it there. He shoved the piece of hull into the water. Dragging it across the island hadn't been easy. Towing it along as it floated wouldn't be as difficult, he thought. He stepped into the water and Sandra followed him. Side by side, they set out toward the unseen mainland.

The bottom of the lagoon gradually shelved off until

the water was about two feet deep. Sandra insisted on taking the lead while Longarm towed the crude raft. "Be careful and don't step in a hole," he warned her.

"I don't intend to," she assured him without looking around.

The water was relatively clear. They could see the bottom in many places. Small fish darted around. Longarm wondered if there were sharks in the Laguna Madre. It was possible, he decided. He kept an eye out for fins.

The sun reflected off the water and became annoying as the morning went on. The heat grew worse. Longarm was very thirsty but tried not to think about it. He continued plodding along in Sandra's wake.

The morning was long and hellish. Every bit of Longarm's skin that was exposed was reddened and blistered by the sun. He and Sandra gasped and slogged on through the lagoon. Even though the water was seldom any higher than his knees, he felt moments of panic when he looked around and saw no land anywhere in sight, only the seemingly endless Laguna Madre. He fought those feelings down and went on.

Several times they had to use the raft to cross areas of deeper water. They stretched out on the piece of hull and paddled with their hands, hoping that their strength wouldn't give out. Each time that the water grew shallower, it was a mixed blessing. At least they could rest a little while they were lying on the raft.

The sun was past its zenith when Sandra pointed and cried out, "I can see it! I can see the mainland!"

So could Longarm. He closed his eyes for a moment and heaved a sigh. With that visible goal in front of them, he knew they could make it.

They set off again, and during the afternoon, as they drew closer to land, Longarm saw the green of vegetation. That meant fresh water. He drew strength from the thought and carried on.

The sun had set and stars were beginning to appear in the darkening sky when the two of them finally staggered out of the Laguna Madre and collapsed on dry land again. No matter how good it felt to rest, Longarm knew they couldn't stay there for very long. They had to find water.

He got up and began searching, and within half an hour he had found a small gully with a trickle of fresh water in it. He fell to his knees and plunged his head into the creek. It took a considerable effort of will to push himself to his feet a few moments later and go back for Sandra. She reacted the same way he had.

By the next morning, hunger was a gnawing problem, but they had rested all night by the creek and drank their fill several times.

Longarm looked around and found a mesquite tree. He picked several of the bean pods and brought them back to Sandra. They ate the beans raw. Longarm had never cared for mesquite beans, but right now they tasted just fine.

He filled his pockets with the bean pods and wished he had something in which to carry water. They would just have to hope that they found another creek.

"It's a long walk to Corpus," he said. "Are you ready?"

She nodded. "As ready as I'm going to be."

They started walking. After a few steps, Longarm reached over and took hold of Sandra's hand.

Late that afternoon, he threw a mesquite branch hard enough and accurately enough to stun a rabbit long enough for him to get his hands on the critter and break its neck. Raw rabbit with the fur still on wasn't much of a dinner, but it beat nothing.

"Reckon we're going back to being barbarians," he said, his mouth red with rabbit blood. "Just like the folks back in the Stone Age."

"No," Sandra said. "The real barbarians are men like Mahone."

Longarm couldn't argue with that.

Clouds had come back during the afternoon, and the wind picked up and had a cool edge to it. Longarm looked at the darkening sky and said, "Looks like another storm blowing in."

"This is the time of year for them. Hurricane season."

They were sitting not far from the shore of one of the innumerable small coves that lined the coast. "Maybe we better move inland a little," Longarm suggested. "Wouldn't want that water to rise up and trap us."

Sandra nodded. "That's a good idea. Now, if I can just find the strength to stand up and walk . . ."

"I know what you mean," Longarm said with a tired laugh.

They leaned on each other as they tramped several hundred yards inland. Longarm didn't know if that would be far enough, but they could move again during the night if they had to.

With the clouds overhead growing blacker, night fell with an appalling suddenness. Sandra huddled against Longarm and said, "I think this is going to be worse than that other storm."

"We'll ride it out," he told her.

The rain started falling not long after that, a deceptively light shower at first. Then the drops came harder and faster, and finally the sky seemed to open up. Longarm and Sandra sought shelter under one of the scrubby mesquites, but it didn't offer much protection from the pelting downpour. They sat there in the darkness, arms around each other, soaked and miserable.

The wind increased to a raging howl. This was more than a simple squall, Longarm thought. It was a damn hurricane.

Suddenly, Sandra screamed and flinched against Longarm. He tightened his hold on her and shouted over the wind, "What is it?"

"A snake!" she cried. "A snake just slithered over my foot. Oh, my God, Custis, it's going to get really bad if the snakes are running!"

Longarm figured they had better get farther inland. He stood up and pulled Sandra to her feet with him. With the wind buffeting them from behind and almost knocking them down, they staggered away from the water. Longarm wondered just how far inland the storm-driven tide would reach.

When he thought they had gone far enough, they collapsed, flopping on the ground and hoping that they wouldn't land on any snakes. The roar of the wind grew even louder, until it sounded like a train about to run over them. That was probably a tornado, Longarm thought, knowing that such twisters were often spawned by hurricanes. Or maybe it was just the wind. He didn't know, didn't care. He covered Sandra with his body and hung on to her, feeling her trembling underneath him. The storm raged over and around them.

Far into the night, the rain stopped and the wind died down to a light breeze. "It's not over," Sandra cautioned when she and Longarm lifted their heads to look around. "This is just the eye of the storm. It'll be back."

Longarm nodded. He knew that. But the respite was nice as long as it lasted.

That wasn't long enough, as far as he was concerned. A short time later, the wind began to howl again, and the pounding rain resumed. Again they ducked their heads to wait out the fury of the storm.

By morning, it was over. The storm was moving on inland, losing strength as it went but still packing winds and heavy rain. Along the coast, where Longarm and Sandra were, the clouds began to break up a little, allowing shafts of early morning sunlight to slant through.

They picked their way back to the cove, avoiding several snakes as they did so. When they got there, Sandra gasped in amazement. The cove was shaped somewhat differently now. The hurricane's power had whittled away some of the coastline.

Longarm spotted something along the shore and frowned. "What's that?" he asked, pointing.

"I don't know. It looks like . . . part of a box of some kind?"

"No," Longarm said, his eyes widening as he realized what he was looking at. "Not an ordinary box. That's one corner of an old chest."

He hurried over to it and started scooping away the sand and crushed shells with his hands. Sandra followed him and joined in the effort. In a short time, they had uncovered the top of the object, which was an old chest with iron straps around it. It seemed to give off an air of antiquity. The locks that held the lid closed had rusted away almost to nothingness. Longarm used a piece of driftwood to knock them away. Then Sandra lifted the lid.

"Oh, my God," she breathed.

The piles of gold coins were tarnished, but it was still obvious what they were. Sandra plunged her hands into the piles and stirred them. Some of the coins farther down were still shiny. They sparkled in the morning sun.

Longarm looked out at the cove and murmured, "Laguna del Diablo." He remembered Cappy Fitzgerald telling him about Bloody Tom Mahone's lost treasure. A hurricane had taken those riches away . . .

And now another hurricane had restored them.

Sandra looked at him. "Custis, is this what I think it is?"

"I reckon so," he said. "Not much else it could be. There should be another chest or two around here. The storm just happened to uncover part of this one."

"But . . . but it's unbelievable . . ."

Longarm shook his head. "Not so much. The original Mahone's treasure had to go somewhere."

"But for us to come along and find it like this . . ."

"History is full of coincidences," Longarm said. "It's just that most of 'em ain't happy ones."

"What are we going to do?"

"It's a cinch we can't dig up all the chests and drag them back to Corpus with us. Best thing to do would be to cover this one up and come back later to get it and the others."

"But who does all this money belong to?"

He smiled. "By right of salvage, I'd say it belongs to you."

"But what about you? What about whoever owns this land?"

"I don't reckon my boss would like it very much if I was to try to claim a bunch of pirate gold," Longarm said with a chuckle. "As for the owner of the land, I reckon we're probably on Captain King's range, and he don't need it near as much as you do. You've got a ship to replace."

"Yes, and a crew." Her face fell. "But I can never replace Cappy and those other men."

"No, I don't reckon you can. Best thing you can do to honor their memory is to go back to sea as soon as you can."

"What about Mahone? Not the real one, I mean, not the one who buried this treasure, but the man who's pretending to be him."

"I know who you mean," Longarm said grimly. "Once we get back to Corpus, he ain't ever going to bother anybody again. I plan to see to that, personal-like."

By mid-morning, they had covered up the chest and Sandra had memorized the surroundings so that she could find it again. After munching on some mesquite beans and drinking muddy water from one of the many puddles left behind by the storm, they started walking again.

The sun wasn't quite directly overhead when Longarm spotted movement up ahead. He grasped Sandra's arm and pointed. "Riders coming," he said.

She sagged in relief and might have fallen if not for his firm hand on her arm. "Who do you think they are?"

"King Ranch punchers more than likely. They're probably aiming to see if they lost any stock to the hurricane."

As the three riders came closer, Longarm and Sandra began to shout and wave their arms over their heads. The horsebackers veered their mounts toward the two people on foot. As they rode up and reined in, Longarm saw that they were dressed in range clothes and were all fairly young. As the cowboys stared at the two bedraggled strangers, one of them said, "Mister, it looks like you and the lady have had a mite of trouble."

"You can say that again, old son," Longarm agreed with a weary grin.

"Can we give you a hand?"

"You boys ride for Captain King?"

"Yes, sir, we sure do."

Longarm had met the former riverboat captain turned rancher. "If you could take us to your boss, I'd be much obliged, and so would Uncle Sam."

The young cowboy's eyes widened. "You're a lawman?"

"May not look like it right now, but I'm a deputy United States marshal. The lady and I have to get back to Corpus Christi as fast as we can." Longarm paused and then added, "We got us a pirate to catch."

Chapter 22

Wearing clean, dry clothes, a borrowed pair of boots, and a broad-brimmed hat, with a Colt on his hip and a Winchester in the saddle boot, riding a sturdy buckskin gelding, Longarm felt like himself again. After everything that had happened, he was somewhat amazed that not only had he survived, but also he actually felt pretty good.

Captain Richard King and his wife had opened their home to Longarm and Sandra. Hot baths, heaps of good food, and some sleep had worked wonders. The rancher had been happy to provide everything they needed for the trip back to Corpus Christi.

Sandra rode beside him on a dun, wearing the same sort of range clothes, borrowed from one of the smaller cowboys who had blushed fiercely at the thought of such a pretty girl wearing his duds. Mrs. King had offered her a dress, but Sandra had chosen the cowboy garb because it was easier to ride in. Just like Longarm, she wanted to get back to Corpus Christi as soon as possible for the showdown.

When night fell, they thought about stopping but decided to push on. Longarm had been over this route before, on his mad dash down to Port Isabel, so he knew the trail. He also knew the shortcut through the Diamond HP that would get them back even faster.

"What if Larribee's not around when we get there?" Sandra asked. "If he gets wind that the law is after him, he may not come back."

"We'll get the fella we're after, don't you worry about that," Longarm assured her.

The sky was overcast again, though not with storm clouds. It was enough to blot out the moon and stars and make for a dark night. Longarm slowed their pace as they rode over Hiram Prescott's range, just to make sure they didn't get turned around.

He estimated that they weren't far from the cove where he had first seen the pirate ship with its ominous black sails, when he heard something that made him rein in and motion for Sandra to do likewise.

"What—" she started to ask before he gestured sharply for her to be quiet. Longarm listened intently. He heard the rumble of hooves, the clash of horns, the occasional lowing bellow.

Somewhere not far ahead, a bunch of cattle were moving.

Longarm remembered the words of Bloody Tom Mahone when the pirate chief had told Mort Shawcross he couldn't pick up any more rustled stock until he had dealt with the *Night Wind*. After dark like this, all the cattle should be bedded down. The only explanation that made sense was that Shawcross and his men were pushing a jag of stolen beeves toward the coast.

Which meant that the black-sailed ship would be there to pick them up.

Longarm's jaw tightened in anticipation. It looked like he and Sandra wouldn't have to ride all the way back to Corpus Christi for the showdown after all.

He leaned over in the saddle and whispered into her ear, explaining the situation in a few quick, concise sentences. "What do we do?" she asked, keeping her voice pitched equally low.

"Can you get to the ranch headquarters from here?"

"I don't know," she said dubiously. "But you know the way there. You can go get help."

Longarm shook his head. "Somebody's got to keep an eye on what's happening up there at that cove. I'll tell you how to find Prescott's place. Get there as fast as you can and tell Prescott to send Chuck Ballinger and the whole crew over here, ready to fight."

Sandra wanted to argue, but it was the only way. When she reluctantly agreed, Longarm gave her directions to the Diamond HP headquarters. She nodded and caught hold of his hand, squeezing it.

"Custis, I know it always seems like I'm telling you to be careful . . ."

He put his other hand behind her neck to steady her as he leaned over even more in the saddle and kissed her. "Get going," he whispered when he took his mouth away from hers.

She turned her horse and walked it away quietly, as Longarm had suggested she do. She didn't heel it into a run until she was out of earshot.

That left Longarm to sneak up on the rendezvous between rustlers and pirates.

He walked his buckskin forward, keeping to a slow, quiet pace. The sounds of the cattle grew louder. Finally Longarm reined in and swung down from the saddle. He slid the Winchester out of the boot and jacked a round into the chamber. Then he tied the horse's reins to a live oak tree and started forward on foot.

He heard men calling softly to each other. Sticking to the shadows underneath the live oaks, he worked his way forward until he could see the cove. Sure enough, the black-sailed ship was there. The cattle were bunched on the shore. Longarm couldn't estimate how many there were; they were just a dark mass to him. Two or three men on horseback kept them contained while other men struggled to set up a ramp leading from shore to an open hatch in the side of the ship. Longarm figured that hatch led into a cargo hold.

He remembered that during the previous conversation between Mahone and Shawcross, someone had mentioned that Mahone was holding a large herd of rustled stock somewhere down the coast. Somebody would have to look after those stolen cattle, and that tied right in with one of the theories that was floating around in Longarm's brain. Pretty soon, he told himself, he was going to have all the answers he needed.

It would take Sandra a quarter of an hour or so to reach Diamond HP headquarters. A few minutes to convince Prescott to send help. With luck, Ballinger and the rest of Prescott's crew would reach the cove in a little over half an hour from now.

Would it take that long to load the cattle? Or would the pirates be ready to leave before then? Longarm was outnumbered by more than ten to one, but if the ship got ready to sail before reinforcements arrived, he would have to do something to try to delay it.

The men who were working with the ramp had it ready. The rustlers on horseback began to haze the cattle up the incline. They went reluctantly. Men stood in the shallow water next to the ramp and used long poles to prod the animals into moving through the open hatch. It was like loading cattle into train cars, Longarm thought. The word "cowpunchers" had come from the fact that men had to use poles like that to keep the cows moving.

The balkier those cows, the better, as far as Longarm was concerned. He stood in the shadows and watched the loading and tried to estimate how much longer it would be before he could expect some help.

He spotted Mort Shawcross on the shore, recognizing the boss rustler by his tall, burly figure. Another man came over to stand with him. Even in this bad light, Longarm could see the long coat and the big buccaneer's hat on the man's head.

The modern-day Bloody Tom Mahone . . . mastermind of the whole thing and cold-blooded killer. Longarm wanted to lift the Winchester and put a bullet through the bastard's head, but he forced himself to wait. He was still a lawman, after all. He had to give even killers a chance to surrender.

But as he remembered the way Mahone had cut down Cappy Fitzgerald, it was hard, damned hard.

The minutes dragged past. More and more cattle were prodded up the ramp into the cargo hold of the black-sailed ship. It wasn't going to take much longer to get them all loaded, Longarm realized. By now, Ballinger and the rest of the Prescott crew ought to be on the way. But would they get there in time?

The soft rustle of a footstep behind him was the only warning he had. He whirled around just as a dark figure loomed out of the shadows. Colt flame bloomed in the darkness as a shot roared out. Longarm felt the wind-rip of the bullet as it passed close by his face.

No need to keep quiet now. The Winchester in his hands cracked as he triggered it.

The gunman who had tried to jump him folded over in the middle. The man's pistol exploded again, but the shot went harmlessly into the ground at his feet. He grated out a curse as he collapsed. His voice was familiar.

Longarm sprang to the man's side, kicked the gun away, and rolled him onto his back. What little light there was showed him the blocky face of Brick Dunn, and Longarm went cold inside as he realized that he had shot one of the Diamond HP cowboys.

But then Dunn's eyes opened and he looked up at Longarm with a hate-filled glare. "Long!" he gasped. "I told Mort you must be . . . some kind of . . . lawman . . . Should've killed you . . . when he had . . . the chance . . ."

Dunn's head rolled to the side and his final breath rattled in his throat. Longarm heard yelling nearby as he straightened from his crouch and stepped behind one of the nearby trees.

Ever since he had discovered the rustling scheme, he had suspected that Shawcross had an inside man on the Diamond HP. Dunn's dying words had confirmed that

178

suspicion. The redheaded cowboy had been working with the gang.

And now Dunn's discovery that the rendezvous was being spied upon endangered all of Longarm's plans. Riders pelted toward the trees where Longarm was hidden to see what the shooting was about. Longarm could have dropped a couple of them, but he turned the Winchester toward the ship instead. He fired five shots as fast as he could work the rifle's lever, aiming at the waterline. If one or more of the bullets punched through the hull, maybe he could keep the pirates from getting away.

Slugs smacked into the trunk of the live oak and showered him with bark. He switched his aim to the muzzle flashes of the rustlers and blazed away at them. He thought a couple of the riders tumbled from their saddles, but he couldn't be sure. Even if he was right, he was still dangerously outnumbered.

But then more shots sounded, coming from a different direction, and a new group of riders raced in with guns blaring. Longarm felt his spirits surge. He heard Chuck Ballinger's voice as the foreman called out orders to the hard-riding, hard-fighting crew with him.

Spooked by the sudden outburst of shooting, the cattle that were still on shore suddenly stampeded, adding to the chaos. As Longarm burst from the cover of the trees and ran toward the ship, he saw Mort Shawcross turn and flee. The boss rustler was trying to make it to his horse, but he was too slow. The stampede caught him. With a hideous scream, Shawcross vanished under the pounding hooves of the runaway cattle.

Longarm looked for Mahone. Had the pirate been trampled, too?

Then Longarm caught a glimpse of Mahone scrambling up a rope ladder to the deck of the ship. The long coat flapped in the air as Mahone threw himself over the railing.

"Cast off! Cast off!" Mahone bellowed, but there was no one to carry out his orders. All the members of the pirate crew had been helping to load the cattle, and now they were busy fighting for their lives against Ballinger and the other cowboys.

The Winchester was empty. Longarm didn't take the time to reload it. He tossed it aside and drew his Colt as he splashed into the water. It was deeper here than he'd expected, but it had to be in order for the ship to get this close to shore. He had to swim the last few feet before he could reach up and grasp the rope ladder.

With water streaming from him, he pulled himself up and began to climb. He had to holster the Colt again so that he could use both hands, but at least he had kept it relatively dry. Hand over hand, he struggled up the side of the ship as the flimsy ladder twisted and turned with him. Finally he reached the rail and grasped it to haul himself up and over.

As he landed hard on the deck, he saw Mahone wheeling a cannon into firing position. The pirate had to struggle with the heavy gun, but he almost had it turned so that he could fire a round on shore. Longarm came up in a crouch and smoothly drew the Colt.

He fired, the bullet glancing off the barrel of the cannon. "Hands up, Mahone!" he shouted. "You're under arrest!"

Mahone turned toward Longarm and roared defiance. His hand swept under his coat and came out with a gun. Longarm fired again, his Colt blasting at the same instant as Mahone's. The pirate's bullet burned along Longarm's forearm, knocking him backward. The Colt slipped out of his hand and skidded off the side of the deck.

He didn't know if he had hit Mahone or not, but the man was still on his feet. And now Longarm was unarmed.

Mahone tossed his own gun aside, though, and reached for the cutlass at his waist. He drew the weapon, with its heavy, curving blade, and charged at Longarm with a curse. Longarm threw himself aside as the cutlass swooped down in a killing strike.

The blade missed him and bit deeply into the deck instead. As Mahone struggled to pull it free, Longarm kicked him in the knee. Mahone let go of the cutlass and stumbled backward. Longarm surged up off the deck and tackled him.

As both men fell, Longarm felt the thick, heavy padding under the long coat. The muted *clang!* as Mahone hit the deck told Longarm that there was a layer of metal in there. He had already figured that out, having seen the way Mahone shrugged off the bullets Sandra fired at him during the attack on the *Night Wind*. Longarm smashed a fist into Mahone's face, knocking the bushy beard askew. He grabbed the false beard and pulled it loose, revealing the handsome features of Harrison Thorpe.

Thorpe wasn't so handsome at this moment, however, because his face was distorted with insane rage. His hand shot up with inhuman speed and closed around Longarm's neck.

"You ruined it!" Thorpe said as he heaved Longarm to the side. "You ruined it all!"

Longarm wound up on the bottom, with both of Thorpe's hands locked around his neck. A red haze filled Longarm's vision. He knew he was on the verge of passing out, and if he did, Thorpe would choke him to death. He reached out to the side, and as he did, he touched the blade of the cutlass.

Struggling to remain conscious, Longarm heaved on the blade. It cut his hand, but it came free. He dropped it, closed his blood-slick fingers around the grip, and swung the blade at Thorpe. The flat of it smacked into the side of Thorpe's head and knocked his grip loose. Longarm shoved the man aside and rolled away, still holding the cutlass.

He came to his feet just as Thorpe charged him with another insane bellow. "Thorpe, look out!" Longarm shouted, but it was too late.

The pirate ran right into the cutlass as the point came up under his chin.

Longarm felt the shock of the impact shiver up his arm. The blade sliced deep into Thorpe's throat, shearing through muscle and bone and arteries so that fountains of crimson spurted from the awful wound, until the point of it ripped out through the back of his neck. Thorpe hung there for a moment, almost decapitated, as his eyes widened and glazed over in death. When Longarm let go of the cutlass and stepped back, Thorpe toppled to the side like a falling tree and crashed to the deck.

Another pirate had met a bloody but richly deserved end.

The details were really pretty simple to clear up once the shooting was over and all the rustlers and pirates had been either killed or captured.

"Mauler Larribee didn't have anything to do with it," Longarm explained to Sandra Nolan as they walked arm in arm along Corpus Christi's waterfront the next day. "I knew it couldn't be him once I figured out Mahone was wearing some sort of bulletproof padding under that outfit. Larribee would have looked even bigger if it had been him. He may be a brutal son of a gun who likes to get in fights, but he's not a pirate. He never even knew what was going on."

"So it was Harrison Thorpe all along," Sandra mused. "But one of his ships was sunk, too, with all its crew."

"Nope. That was a hand-picked crew, and they were in on the deal with Thorpe. They scuttled that ship and rowed ashore in small boats to set up the camp where Thorpe was keeping all those rustled cattle until he was ready to sell them. From what I've heard from the prisoners, he planned to take the cattle to Mexico to sell them. He would've made a pretty good profit from the rustling . . . but not as big as the one he planned to make when he took over all the shipping up and down the Gulf Coast because everybody was afraid of Bloody Tom Mahone."

Sandra shook her head. "Could he ever have done that?"

"Maybe," Longarm said with a shrug. "He'd made a good start on running other folks out of business. He thought he could get away with it, anyway, and that's all it takes once a fella's gone bad."

"I never really liked Harrison all that much . . . but it's hard to believe he was such a killer."

Longarm paused and looked out over the water. "Some of the men who sailed with him said that sometimes he acted like he thought he really was Bloody Tom Mahone, come back to life. I reckon he was more than a little loco, but that didn't make him any less dangerous."

"What now?" Sandra asked.

"Things can get back to normal," Longarm said. "You can recover that treasure and start rebuilding your shipping line. Hiram Prescott gets all his stolen stock back, and he gets a son-in-law to boot, because I hear tell Chuck Ballinger is marrying up with Judith Prescott. It'll be good for the old man to take it easy for a while. He's got a bum ticker. And the Revenue Cutter Service can close the books on that ship they lost. Thorpe sunk it because it came along while he was unloading some of the cattle at the hideout down the coast."

Sandra turned toward him. "And what about you, Custis?" she asked.

"I go back to Denver and see what job Billy Vail's got lined up for me next."

"Not right away, though, surely. I was hoping you might be able to help me dig up those treasure chests."

"Well, I might could wait a day or two to start back," Longarm said with a grin as the warm Gulf breeze blew in his face. "A fella like me, that's probably as close as I'll ever get to a fortune in pirate's gold."

Watch for

LONGARM AND THE OUTLAW'S SHADOW

307th novel in the exciting LONGARM series
from Jove

Coming in June!

Explore the exciting Old West with one of the men who made it wild!

JAKE LOGAN
TODAY'S HOTTEST ACTION WESTERN!